DEADLY FLAME
A WITCH IN THE WOODS

JENNA ST. JAMES

Deadly Flame

Jenna St. James

Copyright © 2025 by Jenna St. James.

Published by Jenna St. James

All Rights Reserved. No part of this publication may be reproduced without the written permission of the author.

This is a work of fiction. Names and characters are either the product of the author's imagination or are used fictitiously, and any resemblance to actual persons, living or dead, business establishments, events, or locales is entirely coincidental.

❀ Created with Vellum

1

"Only three more days until the twins' first birthday," I said, clapping my hands in excitement.

"*I hope Black Forest is ready!*" Needles exclaimed, his wings glowing purple and green.

My flying and talking porcupine partner loved my cousin's twins as much as I did, but he also feared them on some smaller, deeper level. Not that I blamed him. The twins, Cayden and Brooke, were the most advanced werewitches I'd ever come across.

"I can tell they're excited as well," Serena, my cousin and mother to the twin werewitches, said as she glanced down at the stroller she was currently pushing down the sidewalk. She'd just closed her bakery, Enchanted Bakery & Brew, and we were on our way to the candle shop to pick up the twins' special candle to place on top of their cake.

It was mid-August on Enchanted Island. That meant the weather was perfect, the kids were back in school, and parents were back on a set schedule.

"I wish Zoie could have come today," Serena said. "I miss her when she's gone."

"She texted me earlier and said she'd catch up with us tomorrow."

My stepdaughter, Zoie Stone, worked for PADA—Paranormal Apprehension and Detention Agency—as a detective in the Remote Locations Division. She and her roommate, Harlow Grimmson, were the youngest pair of detectives in charge of their own team. Harlow was both a forensic scientist *and* detective. The youngest PADA recruit in history.

I, too, once worked for PADA, but was now retired and working as the game warden for Enchanted Island. That was mostly thanks to my dad, Black Forest King. I'd inherited his ability to talk with plants and animals, which came in handy as the game warden.

"Oh, good," Serena said. "She can tell us all about her latest assignment."

"I know she and Harlow didn't get in until around midnight last night," I said. "PADA wanted to wait to fly them to the island this morning, but Harlow and Zoie were adamant about spending the night in their own beds. So PADA flew them home last night."

"Speaking of Harlow," Serena said as we turned the corner and headed down Black Cat Drive, "I'm so delighted she and Dominic are seeing each other."

At the sound of Dominic's name, the twins started to coo and squeal in their side-by-side stroller. I wasn't sure, but I thought they even high-fived each other…but their sun shields were up, so maybe I'd just imagined it.

"And they are proof opposites attract," Serena went on. "Which is just fabulous."

"I'm still waiting for Harlow to sell ice cream out of his truck," Needles laughed as he settled onto my shoulder.

Dominic Chase was a vampire like Harlow, but that's where the similarities stopped. She was all goth and sarcasm, while he was sunshine and rainbows. She dealt in murder and forensics, while he dealt in throwing parties and driving an ice cream truck.

And yet they worked as a couple.

"Dominic has done such an amazing job with the twins' party," Serena gushed. "He almost has everything finished."

Dominic had moved to Enchanted Island a little over six months ago. He and Harlow had met at the grocery store when they both reached for the last bag of Blood Bites. But we didn't met him until a few weeks ago when the circus was in town and Harlow brought him as her date. It was then we discovered Dominic had a party planning business and had just bought the one and only ice cream truck on the island.

When Serena hired him to plan the twins' first birthday party, I thought it odd to go to such lengths for a children's birthday party—especially when she owned a bakery and knew about parties. But she insisted it wasn't that simple anymore, and she needed help. Grant, her handsome werewolf husband who worked as a detective for the Enchanted Island Sheriff's Department, agreed hiring Dominic would be a good idea.

Even Dad, who was usually picky about who visited Black Forest, was thrilled to meet Dominic. When I first explained to Dominic about my dad—the fact he was a Genius Loci and was an honest-to-goodness tree—he was shocked. But when he met my dad and experienced Dad talking in his head, he was like a five-year-old in a candy store. He must have asked my dad a thousand questions before Harlow finally pulled him away and they left Black Forest.

"There's the candle shop up ahead," Serena said. "I'm glad

Dominic recommended we go with Rosemary Redman for the birthday-topper candle and the commemorative candles."

"What the heck is a commemorative candle?" Needles muttered.

I was just as lost on that deal. "Is it one candle, or…"

"I bought one candle for the cake topper, and two identical candles for the twins to have and put in their room."

"That's the last thing they need," Needles said. *"Those two werewitches do not need a reminder to play with fire!"*

I bit back a laugh. It was common knowledge that Needles thought the twins would burn down Black Forest before their fifth birthday.

"I've not really heard of her," I admitted. "Mom usually makes my practice candles."

Serena laughed. "Mom still makes mine as well. But when Dominic told me about her ability and suggested I scroll her Witchagram account…well, he was right. They are out of this world!"

I glanced at the candle shop up ahead. "Has she been here long?"

"She just moved to this location a few months ago. Before that, she was making the candles out of her home and selling that way. She's only been on Enchanted Island for maybe three years."

I frowned. "And she's a witch? I wonder why I don't know her? Does she participate in one of the other covens?"

There were multiple covens a witch could choose from— everything from singles, to married, to widowed, to the one my family was in…a coven for the original founding families of Enchanted Island. That coven was nearly four hundred years old.

An ice cream truck with the words *Frozen Dreams* slowed down, and Dominic pulled to the curb. Getting out, he gave us a huge smile. "Hello, gang! And my favorite little twins!" He bent down and held out a fist to the babies. And just when I thought I'd seen it all, the twins each gave him a fist bump. "Are you ready for your birthday party?"

The twins' stroller started to levitate, and they both squealed and giggled in glee.

"You two set that stroller down right now," Serena scolded.

"Told ya," Needles whispered in my ear. *"Unnatural."*

Because I knew how sensitive Serena was to Needles' teasing of her advanced babies, I shot him a warning glance.

"Ic! Ic!" the twins shouted.

Since they couldn't say Dominic, they just called the charming vampire Ic. Which he seemed to love.

"Are you getting their candles?" Dominic asked as he pointed to the candle shop just two doors down.

"Yes," Serena said. "I'm so excited to see what Rosemary came up with." She leaned in closer over the stroller, as if telling Dominic a secret. "She has their birthday topper candle ready, but the commemorative candles still need to set. But she was so excited for me to see the topper, she asked me to come in today."

"That's splendid, Serena," Dominic said. "I told you Rosemary was the way to go." He stepped back and slapped the hood of his ice cream truck lightly. "One more round before I park this baby for the night."

"Where do you park it?" I asked.

"In my back alley. Magical Events is my office, and I sleep upstairs in the apartment. The landlord said there was plenty of room out back, and so I park *Frozen Dreams* back there." He winked at the twins as he hopped up inside his ice cream truck and turned on the tinkling music. "Later werewitches."

Cayden and Brooke waved their arms in the air and

squealed…then to my shock, they started blowing Dominic air kisses as he pulled away.

"He gets blown kisses?" I muttered. "I don't get them, and I've changed their diapers, for pity's sake!"

Serena laughed. "Yeah, they've really taken to him."

We stopped in front of Wicked Wicks, and Serena and I each grabbed a twin from the stroller, leaving the monstrous buggy outside.

"Let's go see this awesome birthday candle," Serena said as she pulled open the door.

2

Wicked Wicks was filled with amazing smells and myriad candles, some of which were lit to show customers what enchantment they offered. Tiny floating candles hovered near the ceiling, casting a soft, golden radiance over the shelves. Each wall was lined with custom-built displays, made to look like twisting tree branches, holding candles in every imaginable shape and color. Some were carved to resemble mythical creatures, while others took on more abstract forms, appearing as though they had been sculpted from starlight or spun from the threads of an enchanted spider web. I could smell honey, lavender, and something almost electric that hinted at magic woven into the wax.

"Isn't this place amazing?" Serena whispered.

"Is there a candle that smells like pretzels?" Needles asked, flying up to the ceiling.

Brooke and I headed over to a section of candles that shot out confetti every couple seconds, evaporating before it hit the ground.

"I'm going to ask you to leave one last time," a woman said from one row over. "Then I'm going to have no choice but to call the cops."

I glanced over at the woman speaking and saw she was talking to an angry-looking fairy who looked to be in her thirties. The fairy had long dark hair, black-framed glasses, and generous curves.

Above the section of candles where they stood was a sign that read *Healing-Haven Therapeutic Candles.* Each candle was adorned with delicate labels describing its purported benefit like Relaxation, Energy Boost, Emotional Balance, and Focus.

Unable to help myself, I strolled as casually as I could with a babbling baby in my arms, over to where they stood. Small plaques beside the candles elaborated on their magical properties, with phrases like, "Infused with fairy-touched lavender to ease the soul," and "Crafted under the light of the full moon to restore harmony." At the center of the display was a small glowing fountain surrounded by candles promising healing for both body and spirit.

"This isn't over, Rosemary!" the angry fairy hissed. "You aren't qualified to say your candles have healing therapeutic properties. You're exploiting and preying on others!"

"We're done here, Dana," Rosemary Redman said.

Dana turned and strode down the aisle, stopping when she saw me a few feet away. She scanned my uniform. "Are you a cop?" Before I could reply, she turned and pointed at Rosemary. "You should arrest *her* for making false promises!"

"Simmer down, Fairy," Needles said as he drifted down from the ceiling. *"Or I'll have no choice but to carve out your tongue!"*

Brooke leaned forward in my arms and made a grab at Dana's finger as Needles settled on my shoulder.

"Is there something I can help—"

But Dana didn't let me finish. Instead, she sent one more glare over her shoulder at Rosemary before stomping out the door.

"I'm so sorry!" Rosemary said, plastering a smile on her face. "I'm Rosemary Redman. Owner of Wicked Wicks." Her eyes went wide when she saw Serena sidle up next to me, Cayden on her hip. "Oh, Serena! I'm so glad you stopped by today. The candles are finished!" She gave a small laugh. "Well, one of them is. The two commemorative candles still need to set up, but they'll definitely be ready to pick up before the twins' birthday party on Sunday."

"That's wonderful, Rosemary." Serena glanced over at me and smiled. "This is my cousin, Shayla Loci-Stone."

"It's lovely to meet you," Rosemary said. "Give me two seconds, and I'll get the candle for you." She looked over my shoulder at the young woman rearranging candles across the room. "Pyra, can you give me a hand?"

The young witch turned and nodded. "Sure thing, Rosemary."

As the women hurried to the back room, Serena and I scattered to look around on our own. Shifting Brooke to my other hip, I headed toward a section marked *Spells and More*.

They were colored candles, and under each basket was a label that said what each candle was used for. Green was for prosperity and wealth…red for passion and love…blue for calm and tranquility.

I picked up the red candle to examine it, Brooke clapping in glee.

"You like it?"

Brooke reached out her chubby little hands and tried to grab the candle from me.

"*Absolutely not,*" Needles said, his wings glowing red and gray. "*The last thing that child needs is a reason to play with fire.*"

Laughing, I carefully placed the candle back inside the woven basket.

"So, are we good?" I heard Rosemary say behind the curtained-off area that led to the back room.

"Yeah, Rosemary, we're good."

"You understand why I want you to take things slowly, right? You're new to candle making. It takes time and patience to hone your skill. Your time will come, Pyra, I promise. But not right now. Just stick with me."

"I said it's fine, Rosemary."

"*Doesn't sound like it's fine,*" Needles said from my shoulder.

"Thank you for helping me, Pyra. You can go back to stocking the shelves."

I turned my back on the curtained-off area and pretended to browse some more. When the two women emerged from the back room, I waited until they passed before following after them.

"I'm so excited to see what you came up with," Serena said as she hurried over to meet up with Rosemary. Pyra veered off and went back to stacking shelves.

"So, I did a swirled effect for the candle that goes on top of the birthday cake," Rosemary said as she held up the hand-carved candle.

"It's absolutely beautiful," Serena whispered.

"The predominant colors of the candle are blues and greens," Rosemary went on. "The swirled colors are to represent the twins being one, in both their age and their personality. I've been around the babies long enough to know they share a very special bond."

It was true.

It was like the twins had a language all their own. They used their incoherent babbling to communicate between themselves, which usually ended in disaster because they were concocting some sort of secret spell or using magic when they shouldn't be.

"I went with the blues for Brooke, representing the water, and for Cayden, because I know his middle name is Forest, I went with the greens. There are three different shades of blue and three different shades of green, intertwining."

It was the most beautiful candle I'd ever seen. A blend of water and forest captured in wax. Its base was a deep, swirling blue that transitioned upward into vibrant greens, mimicking the merging of a brook with a forest. Branch-like protrusions extended from the candle's sides, their edges delicately shaped into intricate leaves that seemed to flutter in an unseen breeze. The colors weren't solid but danced in marbled patterns, as though both the water and trees were moving.

"And now for the big reveal," Rosemary said. "As the candle burns, the wax won't melt in the traditional way of one big center burn. Instead, the leaves will burn first and dissolve into the water, as though they are both returning to nature."

"I've never seen anything so beautiful," Serena said, wiping a tear from her eye.

"It is stunning, Miss Serena," Needles said. *"Makes me miss Black Forest."*

"When it burns, it will have a blend of pine, mossy earth, and fresh rain." Rosemary held up the candle a little higher. "Perfectly evoking the union of Brooke's and Cayden Forest's namesakes."

The twins babbled in their own language, clapping their hands and bouncing up and down in our arms.

"I think they approve," I joked.

Rosemary smiled. "Good. Now, the commemorative ones will be similar—they just won't play music."

"Music?" I mused. "The candle plays music as well when burned?"

"Well, more like sounds from the forest—babbling brook, wind through trees, an occasional birdsong, things of that nature." She smiled wistfully. "Infusing music is something my grandmother taught me to do."

"I can't get over how amazing this candle is, Rosemary," Serena said. "I'm so glad Dominic recommended me to you."

Rosemary grinned and carefully placed the candle back in the bag. "As am I." She handed the bag to Serena. "I think I was here maybe a month before he moved into the building next door. He's been a lovely addition to our street of shops."

"I love your therapeutic candles," I said. "I think I'm going to get one for Zoie." I hurried over to the therapeutic section and picked up one labeled Focus before returning to the others.

"Perfect." Rosemary motioned us to follow her as she went behind the counter. "Is there anything else I can help you with before I ring you up?"

"I think that's everything," Serena said.

A cell phone sitting on the counter went off with a notification, and Rosemary picked it up. Rolling her eyes, she set it back down after hitting the screen. I couldn't help but glance down and see a woman's angry face staring back at me.

As Rosemary turned to grab tissue paper from the table behind her, Serena glanced down at the phone, then looked at me.

"That's Faye Ashton," Serena whispered. "She comes into the bakery quite a bit."

Rosemary turned back around, a bundle of colored tissue in her hands. "I was thinking. Pyra or I can text Dominic in the next day or two when the commemorative candles have set and just give them to him. It would save you from having to come back in."

"That's a great idea, Rosemary," Serena said. "I'd appreciate that."

After I paid for Zoie's candle, we waved goodbye to the two ladies and headed outside. I inhaled deeply once more near the door, wanting to take the smell of the candle store with me. Brooke giggled and kissed my cheek.

Once the twins were back in the stroller, I glanced at Serena and frowned. "You okay? You look a little…pale." I bumped her with my hip. "Let me push the stroller. You look exhausted."

Serena nodded, but stepped aside and let me take control of the stroller. "I'm okay. I just worked through lunch and could probably use a little snack." She smiled weakly as we headed down the sidewalk. "I'm making buttered chicken and rice for dinner, so that should perk me up."

I frowned. "Are you sick? Should we move the party?"

Serena shook her head. "No. I'm just tired. I've been working a lot of hours lately." She grimaced and placed her hands on her stomach. "And maybe a queasy stomach."

"Oh, goddess above," Needles said, flipping a somersault in the air, his wings glowing red and orange. *"She's knocked up again!"*

Serena laughed. "No, I'm not, Needles." She frowned and scrunched her nose. "At least, I don't think I am."

Before I could comment, the stroller levitated off the ground, and the twins squealed in glee. A stern-looking vampire passing us shook his head as he strode by, and a young, twenty-something witch covered her mouth as she stared at us, eyes wide.

"You better hope you're not having another werewitch or two," Needles grumbled. *"Black Forest would never survive."*

3

"I thought we'd have grilled halibut and veggies tonight," my husband, Alex, said as I strolled into the kitchen of the castle I now shared with him.

My dad had the large limestone castle—complete with a round turret and dozens of arched windows—built for Mom when he found out she was pregnant with me. Since he couldn't be there for us in person, he made sure we were kept safe and warm. And now it was the home I shared with my husband.

And Needles.

"Sounds wonderful." I leaned in and kissed his cheek. "Wine?"

"Got some white chilling."

"You're perfect," I said, strolling to the refrigerator. "Have I told you that lately?"

Alex grinned as he grabbed the plate holding our halibut. "Bring the wine outside while I put on the fish and stir the vegetables."

"I'll go with the gargoyle," Needles said. *"Make sure he doesn't burn anything."*

As the two left out the conservatory door, I poured two glasses of wine, ran upstairs to change my clothes, then headed outside. The patio was on the west side of the house, the path to Black Forest within sight. At least once or twice a week, I made sure to jog down the path, past my mom's cottage, and into Black Forest to see Dad. Usually, Mom was inside Black Forest as well, so it was a win-win all around.

"How was your day?" I asked, handing Alex a wineglass.

"Happy to say it was pretty quiet." He took a sip and flipped the fish. "Grant can't stop talking about the birthday party. We had a call from Lunger Oakleaf. He says someone is coming in at night and stealing some of his nightshades. So Grant and I are going to drive out to his place tonight and see what we can discover."

I grinned. "A stakeout?"

He laughed. "Not the kind of stakeout you're used to, or I'd ask you to go. I figured you'd go see your dad tonight."

"I was thinking about it."

A few minutes later, Alex plated our fish and veggies while I took a sip of the wine. Shutting off the grill, he handed me my plate. "Let's eat out here."

"What about me?" Needles demanded. *"Where are my pretzel rods?"*

"Over there," Alex said, pointing to a covered dish on the outdoor table.

We sat down at the four-person table, and after lifting the lid off Needles' dish, we got busy eating.

"I think Serena is knocked up," Needles said dramatically as he lounged against the umbrella pole.

Alex choked on his drink. "Excuse me? What did you say? Serena is pregnant?"

I rolled my eyes and shook my head. "No. She's *not* pregnant. At least, she doesn't think she is. She thinks it's stress."

"Mark my words, Princess. Black Forest will never be safe if she is pregnant."

Alex grinned. "Does Grant know?"

"She's *not* pregnant," I insisted. "And stop saying that, Needles. Someone might actually believe you." I set down my wineglass. "She's just tired, is all."

"When can we start placing bets?" Needles asked.

Alex finished the last of his vegetables and pushed back his plate. "I hate to eat and run, but I told Grant I'd pick him up for our stakeout."

Since Serena and Grant lived a mile down the road from us, and we passed their cottage daily, it only made sense for the two to ride to the stakeout together.

"I take it Lunger's place is close?" I mused.

"About ten minutes from here on the east side of the island. Otherwise, I'd just fly out and do the stakeout on my own."

We cleared the table and kissed goodbye. Motioning to Needles, I stepped outside and took off at a leisurely jog down the path toward Mom's and Black Forest.

We were almost at Mom's place when a familiar ball of light came zooming my way, breaking apart just before it reached me. A swarm of lightning bugs zipped and whirled around my head, their glow bright and jubilant.

"Princess! Are you ready for the party?"

"Black Forest King is excited for guests."

"Are the werewitches excited? I bet they are!"

"Did you bring us something sweet?"

Needles leaped off my shoulder and tossed a handful of cotton candy into the air. *"Now, be gone, you ornery fireflies!"*

Giggling and squealing, the two dozen or so fireflies took off toward the entrance of Black Forest, pulling tufts of the sugary strands apart and devouring them...their glowing bodies lighting up like fireworks.

Before long, we came to a stop in front of my favorite pine tree, its towering presence standing sentinel over Black Forest. "Good evening, Mr. Pine. A beautiful night, isn't it?"

"It is, Princess." He carefully lifted one massive branch off the forest floor. *"Black Forest King and your mother are waiting for you."*

I ducked under the raised branch, the fireflies and Needles zipping ahead into the pine's towering canopy.

Entering Black Forest always felt like stepping into another world—peaceful and serene, pulsing with life and magic. Just crossing the threshold gave me an instant surge of energy, a boost of strength that felt like the forest itself was welcoming me home.

Needles let out a whoop and raced forward. *"Come on, Princess!"*

Laughing, I followed him and the fireflies, dodging through the trees, leaping over moss-covered logs, and calling out to the wildlife as we made our way deeper into the forest.

Before long, we reached the clearing where the largest tree in Black Forest stood.

My dad.

Dad was a Genius Loci, the living heart and soul of Black Forest. Thousands of years old, his massive roots rose four feet above the ground, sprawling out like ancient veins anchoring him to the earth. His trunk, impossibly wide, stretched nearly one hundred twenty feet around, and his branches reached so high they disappeared into the canopy.

At the base of his great trunk sat my mom, just as she always did when I visited. Seeing them together brought a familiar warmth to my chest. For many years, Mom had stayed away because she was too heartbroken to visit Dad. But that was the past. Now, she spent a good number of nights out here, the two of them talking and visiting.

"Daughter of my Heart," Dad said as I ran over to one of his massive roots, jumped up, and ran to where Mom sat at the base of his trunk.

"Hey, Dad." I wrapped my arms around him as far as they could reach and rested my cheek against his rough bark. "How are you?"

"Wonderful, now that my two favorite women are here."

"Don't forget about me, Black Forest King," Needles said as he zipped up Dad's branches.

"As if I could, old friend."

I leaned down and kissed Mom's cheek. "You look good."

Mom smiled and patted her hair. "I went into town yesterday and got my hair done for the party this weekend."

I dropped down next to her and rested my back against Dad's trunk. "Are you ready for the party, Dad? Ready to have all the kids running around in here?"

Dad chuckled. *"It has been a long time since Black Forest has had a children's birthday party. All the animals are excited and pitching in to help."*

I grinned at Mom. "I don't think Dominic has comprehended the fact he'll be competing with plants and animals when it comes to making this place sparkle."

Mom chuckled. "I'm so glad he and Harlow are dating. They go together perfectly."

"Perfect like jelly and sardines," Needles snickered from overhead, somewhere in Dad's branches. *"Speaking of warning, have you told them the horrible news?"*

"What horrible news?" Mom asked.

I rolled my eyes and shook my head. "It's nothing."

"Serena is pregnant again!" Needles said as he drifted down to rest on my shoulder.

"What!" Mom exclaimed.

"No, she's not!" I snapped. "Stop saying that, Needles! She's just rundown."

"What is going on?" Dad asked.

"Today, Serena was a little pale and her stomach was upset. She said she'd been putting in more hours at the bakery, she's helping to plan this party, and she forgot to eat lunch on top of it all. Needles just got it in his head she's pregnant, even though she told him she wasn't."

"Mark my words," Needles said, leaping from my shoulder and turning a somersault in the air, his wings glowing red and purple. *"More werewitches are on the way."*

"Are you helping Serena tomorrow?" Mom asked.

"Yes. I'm only working a half day, so Serena, Zoie, and I can meet up with Dominic at Magical Events and finalize everything before they start decorating Saturday afternoon."

"Is Tamara closing the bakery alone?" Mom mused. "Do you think she'll need help?"

I shook my head. "I think she'll be okay." I sighed and stood. "I should head back. Alex is on a stakeout, so I think I'm going to take a bubble bath."

"Take care, Daughter of my Heart. I will see you soon."

Mom stood and hugged me. "Blessed be, Shayla. Love you."

"Love you, guys." I motioned for Needles and the fireflies. "Let's go home."

4

"Thank you again for my candle, Shayla," Zoie said as I exited my battered old Bronco.

"You're welcome. Did you light it?"

Zoie squeezed out of the backseat as I pushed the lever to make the driver's seat spring forward. Serena did the same on the other side of the vehicle. Unhooking the twins from their car seats, we each grabbed one.

"Not yet," Zoie said. "I was going to save it for an extra-stressful day."

Serena popped Brooke onto her hip as I put Cayden on mine. She'd dressed the twins in matching t-shirts proclaiming, *Almost 1*. My cousin was definitely into the whole process of the twins turning one.

Serena shut the door and stepped up onto the sidewalk. "I'm so glad you got back in town just in time for the party, Zoie."

"Arty!" the twins exclaimed simultaneously.

As we passed Wicked Wicks, I had the urge to go inside to show Zoie the interior of the store.

"Let's just pop in and say hi real quick," I said, yanking the door open.

"I knew I should have brought my wallet today," Zoie joked.

"This place would be better if they had candles that smelled like pretzels," Needles grumbled, his wings glowing yellow and green.

Pyra Thornby was standing behind the counter ringing up a purchase when we strolled inside. She looked up and smiled, but I could see the strain and exasperation on her face.

"This is absolutely gorgeous," Zoie whispered, running her hand lightly down a candle shaped like a phoenix.

I smiled politely at the customer exiting the store and made my way to the counter, Cayden babbling on my hip.

"Good morning, Pyra. We just came in to show Zoie around Rosemary's beautiful store." I glanced around but didn't see Rosemary. "I guess she's in the back creating new candles?"

Pyra huffed so hard, her bangs actually moved. "No. I don't know where Rosemary is. I can't reach her." She ran her hands through her hair. "She hasn't come in today, and that's not like her. All of her calls are going to voicemail."

Serena ambled over to us, switching Brooke to the opposite hip. "Oh, no. I hope she's not sick."

"If she was, I'd have thought she'd let me know," Pyra whined. "In another hour, we have one of our regulars coming in to pick up an order that's not even here yet. Rosemary was supposed to bring it with her today. She was finishing it up at home last night."

"How late is she?" Serena asked.

Pyra shrugged. "Like an hour and a half. I know that doesn't seem like a long time, but we've been doing this for years. I open at 8:00, and she arrives no later than 8:30. This isn't like her. At least, not without a phone call to let me know."

I glanced at Serena, then back at Pyra. "We have an appointment next door, but afterward, if she's still not here, I guess we could go by and do a wellness check on her."

"Would you?" Pyra asked. "That would be great. Because, like I said, it's not like her to at least let me know what's going on."

"Do you have her home address?" Serena asked.

Pyra nodded. "Yes. She lives at 39 Fern Drive."

"I know where Fern Drive is," I said.

"Thank you. I was gonna go check on her during lunch, but I didn't want to shut down the store and leave no one here."

"We'll be glad to check on her," Serena assured her.

We said goodbye and exited the store.

"Do you think it's anything serious?" Zoie asked.

I shook my head. "I doubt it. She probably just lost track of time. Maybe she got behind on the candles she's supposed to deliver today."

Serena nodded. "Makes total sense. But just in case, we can swing by, right?"

I held open the door to Magical Events. "Of course."

Dominic's office was stark as offices went. Near the entrance, two modern gray chairs flanked a glass-topped table where potential clients could wait and thumb through event brochures. The walls were painted a crisp white to showcase the myriad colorful photographs on the walls depicting events I assumed Dominic coordinated over the years. Against the back wall, Dominic's desk held a laptop and a framed picture. Three club chairs, upholstered in neon-bright fabrics, were arranged in front of his desk.

"Ladies!" Dominic exclaimed, jumping up from the seat behind his desk. He was dressed in a neon lime-green shirt with orange pants. "Come in. And my favorite twins!"

"Ic! Ic!" the twins cried.

"I think I have everything ready," he said, motioning for us to sit down. "I'm just going over the checklist now." He looked up and smiled. "Oh, and Rosemary told me yesterday she still has candles that are setting. They'll let me know when I can pick them up for you. Should be before the party, though."

Serena nodded. "That's what she told us as well."

"Have you seen Rosemary today?" I asked. "Or spoken with her?"

"Today?" Dominic frowned. "Can't say I have."

We spent the next fifteen minutes making sure everything on the list Serena and Dominic had previously constructed was completed or nearly completed. Tamara—Serena's partner at the bakery—was making the large cake for everyone at the party, while Serena was making their smaller individual ones. Those would be completed tomorrow. Other than that, everything else was pretty much ready to go.

Needles had kept the twins entertained by playing a mix of hide-and-seek and tag with them. But eventually the twins grew bored and started levitating themselves to try to capture Needles.

"Let's take a break for a sweet treat," Dominic suggested. "I have ice cream in cups outside in *Frozen Dreams*."

The twins squealed in excitement.

"Cream! Cream!"

"I don't suppose he has pretzel-flavored ice cream?"

I laughed as Serena and Zoie snatched a baby out of the air. "Needles wants to know if you have pretzel-flavored ice cream."

Dominic grinned as he herded us toward a back door, which I assume led to the alley. "I have Twisted Enchantment. It has chunks of pretzels, ribbons of caramel, roasted pecans, and salted toffee."

"If Harlow doesn't marry him, I will!" Needles did a somersault in the air, his wings glowing purple and green.

Zoie laughed. "I'll be sure to tell Harlow you said so."

"Is that a yes from Needles?" Dominic asked as he held the back door open for us.

"It's probably a yes from all the adults," I said.

The alleyway was spacious, with plenty of parking and two dumpsters for the businesses to use for their respective trash. I noticed one of the bags hadn't made it over into the bin, but before I could use my magic to toss it away, Dominic turned to me, a grin on his face.

"Since Serena and Zoie have their hands full," he said, "Shayla, can you help me carry out the ice cream? I have to warn you, it'll be a little chilly inside. Buford Mapleton, the witch I bought the truck from, enacted a spell that made the freezer stay frozen without the use of a generator, and even the aluminum floor is spelled to stay cooler than normal."

"I don't mind the cool in this heat," I assured him.

"Do you have any with fruit?" Serena asked. "It'll help with the guilt factor if the twins at least have fruit in theirs."

Dominic nodded as he reached up and pulled open the back door to *Frozen Dreams*. "How about Forest Berry Bliss? It has hints of blueberries and blackberries with a twist of citrus as well." He turned and winked at the twins. "Plus, it has magical sprinkles and glitter!"

"I think I want that one," Zoie joked.

Still laughing, I hiked my foot up onto the back step and pulled myself up, following Dominic inside. He was right…it was a little chilly inside. I'd barely righted myself in the back of the truck when I heard Dominic yell out.

It was dim inside…but not dim enough I couldn't see the body on the floor.

A body I recognized.

"I need you to stay right there and not move, Dominic. Can you do that for me?"

"Yes," Dominic whispered, taking a small step backward toward me. His eyes were huge, and he was starting to shake. Shock would set in soon. Turning, I popped my head out the back door. "Serena, keep the kids back."

Needles zoomed over, his wings glowing bright red. *"What's going on?"*

"There's a body inside," I whispered.

"Who?" Zoie asked.

I glanced back inside the truck to the woman sprawled out on the floor, something sticking out of her neck. "Rosemary Redman."

5

I escorted a pale and shaking Dominic out of the truck and motioned for Zoie. "Make sure everyone stays back while I call Alex."

Zoie grimaced. "Needles already suggested I do that. I hope it was okay."

"Perfect," I said. "What did your dad say?"

"He and Grant will be here shortly, and he'd let Doc know. Grant and Serena have been on the phone this entire time as well. They're both pretty upset. Mainly that the twins are here, but she assured Grant the twins didn't see anything."

"Needles, would you stay with Serena, the twins, and Dominic until Alex and Grant get here? I want Zoie inside with me to examine the body."

Needles gave me a salute, his wings glowing gold and purple. *"You got it, Princess."*

Zoie and I left Needles hovering near Serena, who had her phone magically suspended in the air near her mouth as she jostled the twins on her hips. I could hear Grant's voice coming from the phone.

"The first thing I notice is the smell," Zoie said once we were inside the truck. "And for the first time ever, I don't mean a dead-body smell."

I threw up a light orb to illuminate our surroundings. "The beauty of a cold interior. The cold helped to mask any decay, but it will also hinder pinpointing a time of death for right now. Doc will know more about that." I paused. "Okay, what's the smell?"

Zoie closed her eyes and inhaled. "Lavender? But something else as well. A mix of lavender and...?"

I conjured two sets of booties and gloves and passed one to her.

"I'd agree. It's lavender and something else. Of course, Rosemary was a candlemaker, so that's probably not too much of a surprise."

I took a step toward the body, and we both squatted down.

"I'm pretty sure we can identify the murder weapon."

Zoie snorted. "Yes. But what exactly is it? A scalpel?"

"If I had to guess, I'd say it's a candle-making instrument of some kind."

Zoie pointed to Rosemary's hands. "Something is on her skin."

"Finn will be able to identify that."

As if on cue, I heard Alex's deep voice outside, followed by Grant's steady timbre. A few seconds later, Doc poked his head inside the open back door.

"I hear we have a body," Doc said.

Doc Draco was the island's medical examiner and had been for probably longer than my mom had been alive. A dragon shifter, he was a distant relative of Serena's on her dad's side.

"You do." I stood. "It's going to be awfully crowded in here with Finn, Harlow, and you. Zoie and I will get out of your way."

Doc stepped back, and then offered his hand to help Zoie and me out of the truck.

"I'm not sure who's more upset," Finn Faeton said as I stepped down beside her. Like always, she was impeccably dressed. Today, the tips of her hair were dyed purple to match her top and makeup. "Grant for Serena and the twins seeing this, or Harlow for Dominic seeing this."

I bit back a smile as I looked over and saw Harlow doing her awkward best to soothe her emotional boyfriend. I could tell by the mix of exasperation and concern that she was giving it her all. And as a no-nonsense, fact-based vampire-witch who was typically sarcastic, it was obvious she was struggling with Dominic's emotional breakdown.

Serena wasn't doing much better at calming Grant down, either. He had both twins in his arms and was bouncing back and forth between kissing the kids and Serena, as though proving to himself that they were all okay. Needles still hovered near Serena and the twins like I'd asked.

Alex ambled over and gave Zoie and me a small smile. "Shayla, Zoie. What've we got?"

"Rosemary Redman," I said. "She owned the candle shop next door to Dominic—Wicked Wicks. Dominic wanted the twins to have a little treat to keep them occupied during our meeting, and when we came out here, Dominic and I discovered her inside the ice cream truck."

Alex sighed, and ran his hands through his short, cropped hair. "Did you know this Rosemary?"

I shrugged. "Not really. I met her yesterday inside her store. First time I'd ever spoken with her."

Alex nodded. "Okay. Give me a moment."

"You're going to let us investigate, right, Dad?" Zoie asked.

Alex gave her a small smile. "Give me a minute."

Alex turned and walked toward Grant. Needles zipped over to Zoie and me.

"Did you tell him this case should belong to us?" Needles demanded.

I rolled my eyes. "I don't have to tell him, Needles. He already knew what I was going to say."

"We may need a list of reasons this assignment should be ours," Needles went on, as though I hadn't spoken.

Just then, a car pulled in off the side alley and came to a stop. The woman inside hopped out, paying us no mind, a phone to her ear.

"Rosemary, it's Amber. You know, your big sister! Pick up your phone and stop ignoring my calls! We need to talk! I'm outside your place now. I'm coming in."

6

"That doesn't sound good," Zoie whispered.

If the woman headed our way was, indeed, Rosemary Redman's older sister, Amber, then I had to agree with Zoie. This did not sound good at all.

I caught Alex's eyes across the alleyway and moved to intercept Amber Redman before she had time to really process what was going on in the alleyway. She'd just slipped her phone inside her pocket when I stepped in front of her.

"Excuse me," I said.

Amber looked up and frowned. "Yes? Can I help you?" She started to look around. "What's going on back here?"

"My name is Agent Loci-Stone," I said as Zoie and Alex flanked me on both sides, and Needles landed on my shoulder. "And this is Sheriff Stone and Detective Zoie Stone. We'd like to ask you a couple questions."

Amber took a small step backward and shook her head. "I don't...I'm just here visiting my sister."

Alex stepped forward and placed his hand on Amber's arm. "Ma'am, is your sister Rosemary Redman?"

Eyes wide with fear, Amber jerked her arm away. "I don't think I should say anything more. Not until I see Rosemary."

"I'm afraid we have some bad news," I said. "Rosemary's body was found inside the ice cream truck parked—"

"Found her?" Amber snapped. "Is she okay?"

I shook my head. "No. I'm afraid she's dead."

"What? You're lying!" She moved to bolt past us, but Alex held her in place.

"I'm afraid we cannot let you go over there," he said. "We need to preserve the crime scene."

At the words "crime scene," Amber yanked herself from Alex's grasp and bent over at the waist. A heartbreaking moan wrenched from her body. But just as quickly, she stood up, her eyes blazing with anger.

"You're lying! My sister isn't dead. She works—she owns Wicked Wicks. There'd be no reason for her to be inside an ice cream truck." She gave an almost hysterical laugh. "You people obviously don't know how to do your job. If you did, you'd know how silly that was."

Her voice lost its fire as she ended her sentence, and she was once again back to panicking.

"We are sorry for your loss," I said.

Amber slapped a hand over her mouth as tears trailed down her cheeks. "You're sure? There's no way you made a mistake?"

I shook my head. "I'm sorry. No. I'm absolutely sure."

She turned her back on us as she struggled for control.

"I think I'm gonna go see how Dominic is holding up," Needles said as he zipped away, his wings glowing blue and gray.

Amber Redman turned back to face us. "I'm sorry. I'm okay

now." She let out a bark of laughter, but her voice waivered. "I mean, I'm not okay, but I think I understand what you're saying." She ran a hand across her mouth and then swiped at her tears. "What...what happened?"

"It's too early in the investigation to know exactly what has happened," Alex said. "We just received the call a few minutes ago. We have our medical examiner on the scene, but we have yet to speak to him."

"I know Rosemary moved to the island three years ago," I said. "What about you? Did you move here before or after Rosemary?"

"I don't live here. I was just visiting my sister. I've been here about three weeks."

"You're staying with her?" Alex asked.

Amber shook her head and wiped her eyes. "No. I'm staying at The Spellmoore. It's a lovely enchanted inn about fifteen minutes from here."

I nodded. "We know The Spellmoore, and you're right, it *is* a lovely place to stay."

Between Serena's wedding being held there, Zoie having her prom there, and two different investigations that inadvertently involved The Spellmoore, I knew Melody and her enchanted inn quite well.

"I've actually stayed longer than I anticipated," Amber said, "but I'm between jobs right now. Our parents have passed, and I'm not married, so I didn't—" She broke off on a sob. "I didn't really have anything to return to." Tears filled her eyes again. "I guess now that Rosemary is gone, it's just me. I'm the last of our family."

"Your sister had a beautiful shop," Zoie said. "She was a very talented candlemaker."

"Thank you." Amber cleared her throat and swallowed hard.

"She had more talent when it came to designing candles. I was good at enchanting them, but she had natural ability when it came to artistic flair." Amber's eyes cut to the back of her sister's store. "She has a worker. Her name is Pyra. Should I go in and tell Pyra what's happened, or have you already done that?"

I shook my head. "We haven't told Pyra yet. We will do that after we finish here with you."

"Okay," Amber whispered as she wrapped her arms around her body as though hugging herself. "Now what? What do I do next? Do I have to go someplace to look at her and tell you it's her, like they do in the movies?"

"If you'd like," Alex said. "When your sister has been moved to the medical examiner's laboratory, if you would like to come in and—"

"No!" Amber interrupted. "I can't! I don't think I—"

I put my hand on her arm. "You don't have to, Amber. It's just something you can do if you would like. I'm sure Doc has already scanned her fingerprints into our island database, but if you think it might help you in your grieving process, feel free to come in."

"No," she whispered. "You can just tell me whatever you need to tell me after it's done. I'm assuming since you all are here, it's bad. Like someone murdered her?"

I was pretty sure the instrument sticking out of her neck was due to a murder, but I also knew Alex liked to wait for Doc's say-so.

"Possibly," Alex said. "We'll know more once the autopsy is concluded."

Amber nodded. "Okay. Don't forget, I'm staying at The Spellmoore. Do you need my room number?"

"That would be helpful," Zoie said.

Amber let out a shaky laugh. "Is it weird I can't remember? After I said I'd tell you, I can't—"

"Melody and I are friends," I said. "She's the owner of The Spellmoore. I can get with her and get your room number."

Amber nodded and took a step backward. "Okay. That sounds good."

"Are you going to be okay to drive?" Zoie asked. "If not, I can—"

Amber held up a hand and shook her head. "I'm fine. Really. I just want to go back to The Spellmoore."

"Fair enough," Alex said. "Again, we're sorry for your loss."

Nodding, Amber turned around and half-stumbled, half-jogged back to her car. We watched in silence as she slid inside and rested her forehead on the steering wheel. A few seconds later, she started the car and backed out of the alley.

Needles zipped over to where the three of us stood.

"Well, did you make up your mind who's gonna be investigating?"

Alex ran his hands over his face and nodded. "I've given it some thought. Grant has the twins' party in a couple days, and I hate to pull him from the case he should have wrapped up by tomorrow to put him on this case immediately. I could take it, but I know you already know the victim. And if I know you—and I do—you probably already have suspects in mind."

I smiled. "You know me well, husband."

"Yeah, you know us well, Gargoyle."

"So, we can have it?" Zoie asked, her hopeful tone impossible not to pick up on.

Alex nodded. "You guys can have the investigation."

Needles and Zoie fist bumped.

"We'll keep you posted as we go," I promised.

7

"I just don't know what to do," Dominic said. He was standing against the side of his building, head down, shoulders hunched. Harlow was doing her best to console him, but I'd known Harlow long enough to know empathy wasn't her strong suit.

"What you're going to do," Harlow said, "is pick yourself up, dust yourself off, and get back to work."

"She's right, son," Grant said as he jostled Brooke on his hip. "It's not healthy for you to take on the guilt of what has happened."

"He's so sad," Needles said as he settled on my shoulder. *"Even his bright clothes have dimmed a little."*

I bit back a smile. Dominic was known for wearing bright, colorful clothes to match his bright, colorful personality. And I didn't know how, but his clothes *did* look a little dimmer.

Was that possible?

"Who makes your clothes?" Serena asked Dominic.

Dominic gave a small smile and ran his hands down the front

of his shirt. "My cousin, Lourdes. She's a witch on my mom's side. Well, technically, I guess she'd be my second cousin, but we were raised together."

"She's a thread witch?" Zoie asked.

For the first time since we discovered the dead body, Dominic's face split into a grin. "Yes. How did you know?"

"She must enchant your clothes," Zoie said. "I don't know why I never noticed it before."

"I call her my stitch-witch." The smile dimmed a little. "I guess I'm not feeling very festive right now, and my clothes pick up on that."

Cayden and Brooke broke free of Grant's and Serena's arms and hovered in the air near Dominic. Before any of us could react, the twins each laid a hand on Dominic's shoulders.

"Ic! Love!" Brooke exclaimed.

"Ic! Sad!" Cayden added.

Dominic reached out and planted Brooke on his left hip and Cayden on his right. The twins laid their heads on his shoulders and grinned up at him.

"Ick. Love!" they said in unison.

And just like that, Dominic's clothes grew brighter, and a look of pure love radiated from his face. Tears filled his eyes, and he blinked them back quickly as he kissed the tops of the twins' heads.

"I don't know what you guys just did," he said, "but I feel a lot better."

I surreptitiously gave a side-eye look to my cousin, hoping like heck nobody could read the panicked look on my face. Had the twins just given him a soothing spell? How did they know to do that? They couldn't even form complete sentences yet!

"Should I be impressed?" Needles asked. *"Or should I double down on my fear factor?"*

Alex cleared his throat. "Dominic, would it be okay if we asked you some questions?"

"Do you want me to go help Finn process the scene?" Harlow asked. "Or would it be okay if I stayed with Dominic a little longer?"

"Stay," Alex and I said simultaneously.

"Grant and I will just take these little precious werewitches off your hands," Serena said as she grabbed Brooke and Grant grabbed Cayden. "We'll stand over here and give you guys some privacy."

Once Serena, Grant, and the twins stepped away, we closed ranks even more around Dominic.

"We won't be too long," Alex said. "Shayla said you were the one who opened the back door to the ice cream truck. Is that right?"

Dominic nodded. "Yes."

"So, it wasn't locked?" Alex asked.

"No. I honestly never lock it. I've never had a problem before."

"What about noise," I said. "Do you remember hearing anything in the alleyway last night or early this morning?"

Dominic shook his head. "No. But again, I'm not sure I would have heard much from my upstairs apartment or inside the building."

"When was the last time you had *Frozen Dreams* out?" Zoie asked.

"Yesterday." He pointed to me. "After I talked with you guys on the street, I made some rounds, and then parked it out back here and went inside to finish working in my office. Because I wanted to make sure I had everything ready for the twins' party and our meeting this morning, I didn't take the truck out today. I just came downstairs this morning around 8:00 and started to work."

"Did you know Rosemary?" I asked.

Dominic shrugged. "I'd see her and her worker occasionally, and we waved and stuff, but I never really chatted with her or anything." He turned to Harlow, his eyes wide. "You don't think someone did this to send me a message, do you?"

Harlow arched a brow. "What kind of message, Dominic? 'Stop selling ice cream, or you'll be the next frozen popsicle.' That kind of message?"

It's pretty catchy," Needles said.

"And who's sending the message?" Harlow demanded. "We only have one ice cream parlor around here."

Dominic sighed and ran his hands through his hair. "I guess you're right." He glanced over at his ice cream truck. "Poor Rosemary."

"Can I see whoever's working the case?" Finn hollered from the back of the ice cream truck.

I glanced at Alex, and he gave me a small smile and waved me away.

"Zoie and Needles with me," I said.

We strolled over and climbed inside the truck.

"I'm thinking the shiny substance is beeswax," Finn said. "I think it smells of lavender and sage. But I want to run it through the lab."

"I'm going to need more time to work out time of death," Doc said. "With the temperature in here being altered, I can't give you a specific time, Shayla. Sorry about that. Hopefully, I'll have something for you after I complete the autopsy."

I nodded. "I figured as much. Just keep me posted on all your findings."

We climbed out of the truck, and Serena waved us over. "I

think I'm going to take the twins home. I know they seem fine, but Grant and I...we're not fine."

"You guys take all the time you need," Alex said. "I've got Shayla, Zoie, and Needles on this. Grant, you worry about your family."

Grant nodded and slapped Alex on the shoulder. "Thank you. I'm going to take you up on that offer. I'll be back in the office later this afternoon."

"And don't worry," Dominic said. "I'm going to push through and give the twins the best possible birthday their little minds have ever imagined."

"Seeing as how they're a year old," Needles whispered in my ear, *"I can't imagine it'll be too difficult."*

8

I opened the front door to Wicked Wicks and stepped inside. Scanning the store, I saw Pyra standing by a wall of candles, some kind of circular light hovering magically in the air near her face. She was talking to no one I could see.

"What is that?" I asked, gesturing to the circular light.

"It's a ring light," Zoie said. "People use them as a filter so they look softer on video."

"I don't want to look softer. I want to look fierce, like the warrior I am."

Pyra reached up and pushed a button on the phone that was inside the circle.

"Why is her phone up that high?" I asked. "You'd think she'd strain her neck looking up like that."

Zoie laughed. "Wow. You really need to get out more, Shayla. Everyone knows you tilt the phone up like that, so you look better on camera."

Pyra hurried over to us. "Hello. I was just practicing. Rosemary usually does the videos, but since she isn't here today, I thought I'd do it. She says it's important to post every day around the same time."

"She seems a mite eager," Needles scoffed.

"Pyra," I said, glancing around the empty store, "we need to speak to you for a moment."

"Of course. What's up? Were you able to check on Rosemary already?"

I shook my head. "No. But this *is* about Rosemary."

"Okay. What's up?"

"I'm afraid we found Rosemary's body stashed in the ice cream truck out back."

For a few seconds, Pyra's face didn't change. Slowly, her brows drew down, and she frowned. "What? I don't understand. What are you saying?"

"I'm afraid Rosemary Redman is dead," I said.

Pyra shook her head. "That can't be. I just spoke with her last night." She rested a hand on her chest. "Are you sure? She's… dead?"

Zoie nodded. "I'm afraid so, Pyra. I'm sorry for your loss."

"What? That…*what?*" Pyra stammered.

I placed my arm on the young girl and steered her over to the counter so she could lean against it.

"Zoie and I need to ask you some questions."

"Uh, okay, I guess."

"When was the last time you saw or spoke to Rosemary?" I asked.

"Like I said earlier, last night around 5:00. She said she had a couple things she needed to do around the shop, so she was just going to stick around for a bit. I didn't think anything about it."

"And you opened this morning, right?" I asked.

"Yes. She wasn't supposed to come in until 8:30. But when

she didn't show, I got worried. Especially since my phone calls were going to her voicemail."

"Had she been having problems with anyone?" Zoie asked. "Maybe someone harassing her or causing her some distress?"

I immediately thought back to the angry woman in the shop yesterday.

"Well, there's Dana Dunphrey," Pyra said, "but you probably heard that exchange yesterday."

I nodded. "I did. Do you know what the disagreement was about?"

"Not really. Rosemary is pretty—I mean, Rosemary was pretty closed-mouthed about it. And that was the first time that woman ever came into the shop to yell at us."

"Is Dana a candlemaker?"

"No. She's a holistic life coach. But I don't know why Rosemary was seeing her, or what exactly Dana's beef was with Rosemary."

I nodded. "Okay. Anyone else you can think of?"

Pyra bit her lip and looked away, and I could tell she was struggling with what to say.

"Pyra," Zoie said, "someone hurt Rosemary. If you know something, we need to know."

"She's had some words with the Ashtons. They're a mother-daughter team, Alice and Faye. They're not exactly fans of Rosemary's."

I frowned. "I know that name."

"They make candles as well," Pyra said. "In fact, they have a store on the south side of the island."

Zoie leaned against the counter. "So Rosemary didn't get along with Alice and Faye Ashton?"

"Nope."

"Why is that?" I asked.

Pyra rolled her eyes. "It's a very long story. I wouldn't even know where to start."

I gave her a small smile. "No problem. I'll ask them myself."

"Anyone else?" Zoie asked.

Pyra shrugged and shook her head. "I don't think so. Not that I can think of off the top of my head, anyway."

"Let's talk about you," I said. "Where were you last night from the time you left here, until you came into the shop this morning?"

Pyra's nose curled in disgust as her mouth dropped open. "Do you think I hurt Rosemary? That I killed her and stuffed her in the ice cream truck outside?"

I shook my head. "No."

"Yep, that's exactly what we think," Needles said.

"That's not what we're saying," I said, doing my best to ignore Needles. "We just need to know where you were at all times, so we can cross you off our list when the time comes."

"Fine," Pyra huffed. "Like I told you, I left here around 5:00, picked up dinner at Boo Burgers, and then went home. I ate, watched some TV, and then went to bed."

"Do you live alone?" Zoie asked.

"No. I have a roommate. She works the night shift, which means she doesn't get home most nights until 11:15 or later."

"What time did you go to bed?" Zoie asked. "Did you see your roommate come home?"

"Yeah, but only for a few minutes. I knew I had to get up early and open the shop. So I'd say I went to bed around 11:30."

I crossed my arms over my chest. "Do you know what will happen to the store now that Rosemary is dead?"

Pyra threw up an arm and huffed. "I don't know." Her eyes went wide. "Does her sister know? Rosemary's sister is visiting right now. Someone needs to tell her."

"We've already informed her," I said.

"Then, as far as what happens to the store, someone will need to figure that out. I don't know if Rosemary willed it to her sister or if Rosemary even had a will. We were friendly, but we weren't like besties or anything."

I slipped out my phone and pulled up my photos. Doing my best to crop out Rosemary's neck so Pyra could only see the murder weapon, I turned my phone to face her. "Do you know what this is?"

Pyra leaned forward and squinted her eyes, then reeled back in horror. "Oh, my goddess! Is that what I think it is?"

"What is it?" I asked.

"Is that the murder weapon? I mean, you're basically telling me Rosemary was murdered, right?"

"It's a little early in the investigation to—"

Pyra threw up a hand as if to ward off my words. "Whatever. Yes, I know what that is. It's a wick dipper."

I frowned. "Wick dipper?"

Pyra turned her head and blew out a breath. "We usually sell a wick dipper in a set. You'll have a snuffer, a wick dipper, and a wick trimmer. All three of those help keep your candle in the best condition it can be."

"What exactly does a wick dipper do?" Zoie asked.

"Let's say your candle is lit. You don't lean over and blow a candle out because that can cause splatter or an uneven burn pattern. Instead, you take the wick dipper and press down on the wick until the flame goes out in the wax."

"Why does that help the candle?" Zoie asked.

"Because now you have wax on the wick. It seals it and keeps it from smoking when you relight it. It also helps preserve the wick for longer use."

"And you sell these sets here in the store?" I asked.

"Oh, yes. The sets are very popular. You can pretty much find them in any candle-making store."

I slipped my phone back inside my pocket and looked toward the back room. "I'd like to see Rosemary's office, please."

The front door opened, and a customer walked in.

"What do I do?" Pyra asked. "Do I tell them to go away, or do I wait on them?"

"Go ahead and wait on them," I said. "We can find our way to Rosemary's office."

As Pyra hurried away to greet the customer, Zoie, Needles, and I made our way to the back room.

9

Rosemary Redman's office was lined with shelves filled with candles, candle-making supplies, and myriad books. On the opposite side of the small room, pushed up against one side, was a desk, chair, and an iPad.

"Only one drawer in her desk," I said. "Shouldn't take long to go through."

Using my magic, I pulled the drawer open and peered down. Three or four pieces of paper lay inside. Again, using my magic, I levitated each of the papers into the air and read aloud. *"Don't think I have the power to ruin you? Ask Grilla Truehart the kind of power I hold!"* I set it down and read the next note. *"Tradition is king. You can't come in here throwing all that out the window."*

"Are any of them signed?" Zoie asked.

"Alice Ashton," I said. "At least, the first two are signed by her. This last one isn't signed at all, but it lets us know why she stayed behind last night."

"Why?" Needles asked.

I read aloud from the note. *"Meet me at Wicked Wicks at 7:30. I'll bring dinner. We need to talk."*

"Of course it's not signed," Zoie said. "That would be too easy." She conjured an evidence bag and used her own magic to place the notes inside. "Hopefully, Finn and Harlow are still out back, and we can give them these." Once the notes were bagged, she motioned me over to one of the bookshelves. "I think I might have found a grimoire." She levitated the leather-bound book off the shelf so I could see it…using her hand to flip the large pages.

"Looks like you're right." I sighed. "Harlow and Finn may be here a while. I don't think the store has to shut down, but I think this area should be processed and warded. Maybe the girls can find an opened wick dipper set back here." I conjured up another evidence bag. "And until Alex tells me what to do with what looks like a family grimoire, I guess it goes into holding."

Pyra was still helping the customer when we walked back into the store. I caught her eyes and told her not to go into the back room, then headed out the back door.

As I stepped outside, I had a sudden thought. "Look at the trash over by the bin," I said to Zoie. "I noticed it earlier. What if Rosemary was taking out her trash last night when she was taken by surprise?"

Zoie nodded. "It makes more sense as to why she was stashed in the ice cream truck instead of being killed inside and just left there. Maybe her killer attacked her back here. Rosemary dropped the trash, the killer panics, sees the truck, and puts her in there."

"I'd say that sounds like a pretty solid theory," Alex said. "I'll have the trash collected for evidence."

I turned and smiled at my handsome husband. "I'm surprised you're still here."

Alex put his hands on his hips. "I thought I'd stick around until Finn and the others left."

Zoie and I both held up our evidence bags.

"What is it?" Alex asked.

"Some notes from a possible suspect," Zoie said.

"And I have what looks like a family grimoire," I added. "Not sure what you wanted to do with it."

Alex frowned. "I don't want it to be stashed in an evidence room forever, but until we know more about what's going on here, I say we keep it secure."

I nodded. "Agreed. I was going to ask Finn and Harlow to weed through Rosemary's office. Ward it up until the crime is solved. I don't think we need to close down the shop."

"I can agree with that," Alex said. "Plus, I'll drive by Rosemary's house and make sure her house is locked up nice and tight."

"Good. I need to talk with Dominic again real quick."

Alex held out his hand. "I'll give these to Finn and Harlow, and let them know you'd like the office gone over as well. Dominic went back inside his building."

We passed our evidence off to Alex, and the three of us made our way inside. Dominic was sitting at his desk, staring off into space.

"Hey, Dominic," Zoie said. "How're you doing?"

"He looks awful," Needles said, his wings glowing blue and gray.

"Feeling pretty blue, to be honest." He motioned to a candle on his desk. "I'm hoping this will be a little bit of a pick-me-up."

"I just have a quick question," I said. "What did you do last night from 5:00 until 8:00 this morning?"

"Let's see. I had dinner with Zoie and Harlow at their house around 6:00 Then we all watched a movie. Zoie went to her room around 9:00 when the movie was over." Dominic's neck and cheeks flushed as he cleared his throat. "I stayed a little longer, hanging with Harlow. You know, just..."

I smiled. "It's okay. You can just tell us what time you left."

"Probably twenty or thirty minutes after Zoie went to bed." He glanced down at his desk, unable to meet my eye. "Harlow and I just kind of hung out, you know?"

"His face is about as red as that candle he's burning," Needles snickered.

"What time did you get home?" I asked.

"I think about 9:30 or 9:45. The sun was down, so it was pretty late."

"What'd you do when you got home?" Zoie asked.

"Oh, nothing. I just went to bed."

"And you never saw or heard anything?" I asked. "You didn't get up in the middle of the night, maybe to get a drink of water or go to the bathroom?"

Dominic shook his head, looking like he wanted to cry. "No. I'm a pretty solid sleeper." He gave me a half-smile. "Guess you could say I sleep like the dead."

Any other time, a vampire saying that would have made me laugh.

Needles dropped from my shoulder, laughing so hard he had to clutch his stomach, his wings glowing purple and green. *"That was a good one!"*

I smiled at Dominic. "That's all we need."

Dominic leaned over the candle and waved his hand back and forth over the flame, inhaling deeply. "Yeah. Not helping."

10

"I want to make a quick stop," I said to Zoie and Needles as we stepped outside onto the sidewalk in front of Magical Events. "Rock of Ages is next door to Wicked Wicks. Let's see if Calypsis heard anything."

"Who's Calypsis?" Zoie asked. "The owner?"

"Yes. She and GiGi grew up together."

Alex and I were supposed to have dinner with GiGi and her fiancé, Byron Sealy, tonight at High Seas Bar & Grill. I'd have to remember to call and cancel. Which she wouldn't like. Especially when she found out I was cancelling because I was leading the investigation into the latest murder. She'd demand all the details.

I held open the door to Rock of Ages for Zoie and followed behind her, Needles leaping from my shoulder.

"It's so shiny!"

"It is," Zoie whispered in awe as she glanced around the room. "And can I just say I want every single item in this shop?"

Rock of Ages was a kaleidoscope of color and magical

charm. Crystals, rocks, and gems of every shape and size lined the wooden shelves. Calypsis didn't believe in overhead lights. Instead, she used the natural lighting from the picture window and enchanted lanterns to set the shop ablaze. Incense burned in ornate holders shaped like mythical creatures, filling the air with the earthy scent of sage, patchouli, and sandalwood.

"It's an earthy smell for sure," I agreed.

A large amethyst geode dominated one corner of the room, while a black cauldron near the counter bubbled gently with what appeared to be some kind of potion. The wooden floor creaked underfoot as I ran my hand over a moss agate stone. It was my favorite stone—my wedding ring was proof of that.

Calypsis stood behind the counter, wrapping a bundle of dried lavender and sage. Her silvery hair, braided and adorned with tiny charms that jingled softly when she moved, caught the light from the enchanted lanterns above. She looked up, her sharp green eyes lighting with recognition. "Shayla, my dear. To what do I owe the pleasure?"

I smiled politely, moving closer. "I need to ask you a few questions, Calypsis. It's about last night."

Her brow furrowed, but she nodded, setting the bundle aside. "Of course, ask away." She held up a crooked and wrinkled finger. "But first—how is your grandmother? I was thrilled when I heard she was getting married again."

"She's great, Calypsis."

She narrowed her eyes as Needles landed on the counter in front of her. "Is that the porcupine who used to tag along with you when you were a kid? The one your father sent?"

"Darn right, it is!"

I smiled. "It is. His name is Needles."

Needles gave Calypsis a small bow, his wings glowing purple and green.

"How delightful!" the older witch exclaimed. "And the beautiful young lady with you? Is that your stepdaughter I've heard so much about?"

"I am," Zoie said. "My name is Zoie Stone."

"Strong name." She gestured around her shop. "Just like the stones I sell."

"Your shop *is* lovely," Zoie said.

Calypsis frowned and stared at Zoie. "You will take a protection stone with you when you leave. Maybe black tourmaline? Yes. You will take that stone with you and keep it with you at all times."

Zoie shook her head. "Oh, no. It's—"

"I insist." Calypsis narrowed her gaze. "You do what Shayla does? You chase bad supernaturals?"

"I do," Zoie admitted.

"I can sense that. Therefore, you will choose one."

"I can't decide if she's being pushy or foreshadowing something," Needles said. *"Either way, it gives me the creeps."*

"Thank you," Zoie said. "I'll do that.

Calypsis nodded once. "Good. Now, what questions did you want to ask me, Shayla?"

"Did you close the store yourself yesterday?" I asked.

"Yes, it's just me working here for now," she replied. "I closed at 4:00 sharp and opened again this morning at 9:00. Why?"

"There's been an incident next door," I said. "Is there anyone in the apartment above your store?"

She shook her head, a few silver charms chiming with the motion. "No one is renting the apartment above right now. It's been vacant for two months." She paused and studied me. "What's going on?"

I hesitated, but knew she'd hear eventually. "Rosemary Redman, the shopkeeper next door, was murdered."

Calypsis' hand flew to her chest. "By the goddess! If there's anything I can do, please let me know."

I nodded. "Did you know her?"

"Only in passing. She kept to herself, mostly."

"Thanks for your time, Calypsis." I slid my business card across the counter. "Call me if you hear anything, would ya?"

"Of course. And give GiGi my best. I missed our last coven meeting. I was feeling a little under the weather." She clasped her hands and stared down at Zoie. "Now, before you go, we need to get you a protection amulet."

"I'm the one who should get one. I have her and *Harlow to protect!"*

Ever since Needles started accompanying Zoie and Harlow on their Remote Locations assignments from PADA, he'd been losing more and more quills. He joked it was one thing to protect me, but having to care for *three* hard-headed women was about to do him in.

"How about this?" Calypsis mused as she handed Zoie a bracelet. "It has both black tourmaline and tiger's eye. Perfect for you."

"I love it," Zoie said, slipping the bracelet on. "How much?"

"No. It is a gift for you." She picked up Zoie's hand and stared into her eyes. "You have a protection around you I cannot describe…" She glanced at me and nodded. "Or maybe I do understand. But this will just enhance the protection that Black Forest King has already gifted you."

Tears filled Zoie's eyes. "Thank you. I'll cherish this and wear it."

"See that you do, little witchy gargoyle." Calypsis dropped Zoie's hand. "See that you do."

11

"Because I want to follow every lead," I said as we left Rock of Ages and headed for the Bronco, "let's stop by Ice Scream, You Scream."

Not that I thought for one minute the owners of the ice cream parlor, Gladys and Charlie, had anything to do with Rosemary's murder...but Dominic had put it out there when he mentioned someone sending him a warning.

"Do you think Serena and Grant are going to be okay?" Zoie asked as she buckled her seatbelt. "I mean, obviously this didn't scar the twins, but I'm not so sure about Serena and Grant."

I grinned as I pulled out onto the street. Ice Cream, You Scream was located in the middle of town on the main drag—which meant just a few streets over. "They'll be fine. I think they're more freaked that the twins *are* okay with everything, even offering Dominic comfort. They're barely 363 days old. That's pretty powerful stuff for babies."

"Which reminds me, did you notice how fast Serena jumped

on that ice cream?" Needles said from the backseat. *"You know what they say about ice cream and pickles!"*

I snorted. "We *all* jumped on the ice cream offer, Needles."

"Just sayin'." Needles shoved a pretzel rod in his mouth and chewed.

"What did I miss?" Zoie asked.

"Needles has it in his head Serena is pregnant."

Zoie gasped. "Seriously?"

I slid my gaze to her. "Don't say anything to Serena until she says something first."

Zoie made as if she were locking her lips and throwing away the key. Then squealed. "But, yay, if it's true!"

I turned left onto Charmed Street, and then parked along the curb a few doors down from the ice cream parlor. We'd just stepped onto the curb when Mrs. Mystic waved her hand in greeting. She had her youngest on her hip.

"She doesn't have her fifty kids with her, does she?" Needles grumbled as he settled on my shoulder, looking around.

"Good morning, Mrs. Mystic," I said. "How are you today?"

"Well, all the other kids are back in school, so it's a blessed day for me and the baby." She sighed. "They span elementary to high school. What were Mr. Mystic and I thinking?"

"I've wondered the same thing," Needles said.

Zoie giggled and then hid it with a cough.

"Well, you have a lovely day, Mrs. Mystic." I waggled two fingers at the baby. "Bye."

I held the parlor door open for Zoie and followed behind her. It was nearing one o'clock, but since kids were in school for another two-and-a-half hours, the store was practically empty.

"Good afternoon," Gladys said from behind the counter. "We have—oh, hello, Shayla. And Zoie, isn't it?"

"That's right, Mrs. Lunaman," Zoie said.

She clapped her hands together and pointed to her display case. "What can I get you? Today's specials are on the board."

I had to smile because the daily specials were almost always the same flavors every day—unless it was a holiday and they made something special.

Oreo Eye Scream—vanilla ice cream with chunks of Oreos and edible eyes. Brownie Bug Bites—chocolate ice cream with bits of brownies and edible gummy bug parts. And Blood Bath Crunch—vanilla ice cream with cherries and walnuts.

"Not today, Gladys," I said. "I'm afraid we're here in an official PADA capacity."

Gladys gasped as her hand flew to her chest. "Oh, no. It's not Charles, is it?"

"No, ma'am," I said. "It has nothing to do with your family. It's about Dominic Chase and Rosemary Redman."

Gladys frowned. "I know that lovely Dominic boy. We just think the world of him! So creative." She shook her head. "But I don't know Rosemary. Does she have an ice cream store as well on the island?"

I shook my head. "No. She has a candle store."

"Okaaaay," Gladys said, drawing the word out. "I'm with you so far."

"Earlier this morning, the body of Rosemary Redman was found in Dominic's ice cream truck. She'd been murdered."

"Oh, that poor boy! And poor Rosemary. Now that you say who she is, and that she had a candle shop, I realize she had the store next door to Dominic." She reached inside the display case and started dishing out ice cream in a waffle cone. "Dominic is such a sweet boy. The first week he bought the truck, he parked it in front of our store and invited us out to see it. We didn't have the heart to tell him we knew about the ice cream truck. Buford had been running it for years. So Charles and I oohed and aahed all over it." She handed Zoie the cone. "Oreo Eye Scream. I remember you ordered it the last time you were in. How about you and Needles? Can I interest you in some Blood Bath Crunch?"

I nodded. "That would be great, Gladys. Thank you."

"She needs to get with Dominic," Needles grumbled as he settled on my shoulder. *"He at least has pretzel bits in his stuff."*

"Now, where was I?" Gladys mused as she scooped out a huge portion and set it on top of the cone. "Oh, yes. So now that you say who Rosemary is, I vaguely recall running into her the last couple years. That's just awful about her death."

"You understand why I need to ask you some questions, right?" I mused as I took the cone from Gladys. "You guys own an ice cream parlor, and a body was stashed in the back of your competitor's ice cream truck."

Gladys waved her hand dismissively in the air. "Dominic isn't competition, but I understand. What do you need to know, Shayla?"

I took a little nibble of the ice cream. "I just need to know where you were last night from 5:00 until early this morning."

"Well, as you can see, we're not doing a whole lot of business right now. But from four o'clock on, we're usually packed—what with summer coming to an end, kids out of school, and parents wanting to get out while it's still nice. So, last night, Charles and I stayed open and didn't close the ice cream parlor until around 8:00. We locked up, went home, and I heated us up some dinner. Then we fell into bed." She sighed. "I hate to admit it, but we're getting older. Not sure how much longer we'll be able to hold on. Our daughter and grandkids fill in now and then for us, but before long, we'll need to have a serious conversation." She winked. "Mainly between me and Charles. Neither of us wants to give it up."

Zoie took a small bite of an Oreo. "With delicious ice cream like this, I hope you never quit."

"You're too kind."

"What time did you get up?" I asked.

"Let's see. I always get up first. I think I was up by 7:00 this morning. I put on some coffee for Charles and made him his favorite—scrambled eggs and toast. We hung out around the house until it was time for me to open the parlor around 10:00 this morning."

I nodded. "Okay, that should be everything, Gladys. Thank you for answering my questions and understanding why I needed to do it."

"Of course." She leaned over the counter. "And don't worry. If I hear anything, I'll be sure to give Opal a call down at the sheriff's station."

12

"Now that we've established the Lunamans' alibis," I said, slamming the door shut on the Bronco, "let's go question our other potential suspects." I pulled up the interactive app that showed me all home and business addresses for the island and plugged in Dana Dunphrey's name. "Looks like she's near Wicked Wicks, and she lives above her office."

Dana's office was just two blocks away on the same street as Wicked Wicks and Magical Events. Parking along the curb, we got out and made our way toward a building sandwiched between two others. There was no sign hanging either by hook or magical enchantment above the store. Instead, the only way passersby could tell what was inside was the phrase "Holistic Life Coach" stenciled across the picture window.

A note on the door announced Dana would be back at 1:30. I glanced at my watch. It was now 1:22.

"There's a novel idea," Needles said. *"Lunch. I'm starving here, Princess."*

"I wouldn't say no to some food either," Zoie said.

"Can I help you?" a voice asked behind us.

Zoie and I turned, and I immediately recognized the woman from yesterday—Dana Dunphrey. She was holding a brown paper bag in her hand.

"Dana Dunphrey?" I asked.

"Yes. If you're here to speak to me, please make an appointment. I have someone arriving in ten minutes."

I gave her a small smile. "This won't take long, but it might be best if we go inside."

From her put-out tone, I got the feeling she didn't recognize me from the candle store yesterday.

"Is this really that important? I have a client coming soon."

I nodded once. "Like I said, we'll be fast."

Zoie and I stepped to the side as Dana waved her hand in front of the door, disengaging the lock. "Come in."

"She seems pleasant," Needles said. *"I can understand why she went into life coach as a profession."*

We followed her inside, Needles immediately heading for the ceiling.

What the room lacked in space, it more than made up for in ambiance. There were numerous pothos and spider plants, a healthy-sized mother-in-law's tongue, and three orchids scattered around the room between healing crystals and numerous candles. The only furniture in the room was a desk and chair next to a filing cabinet in the back. The center of the room held a chair and a chaise lounge. At the front, near the door and window, a small tea set and three self-help books sat on a wooden coffee table.

"Your plants are lovely," I said as I shut the door behind me.

"Thank you. I usually recommend my clients acquire a few to nurture and love."

I closed my eyes, reached out, and opened myself to the

emotions inside the room. It didn't take long for me to learn the plants, overall, were healthy and happy.

"Now, what is this about?" Dana asked as she walked to the back of the room, tossed her paper bag onto the desk, and sauntered back over to Zoie and me.

"My name is Agent Loci-Stone, and this is Detective Stone. We are—"

"I know who you are," Dana interrupted. "I may have only lived on the island for eight years, but people talk."

"You should see if she's heard of me, Princess," Needles said. *"I'm sure my legendary status as a fierce warrior precedes me."*

"I believe I saw you yesterday inside Wicked Wicks," I said. "It looked like you were having words with Rosemary Redman."

Dana's nostrils flared, and her lips pursed. "Yes, you could say I was a little upset."

"Can you tell us why?" I asked.

Dana paused and looked between Zoie and me. "Let's just say Rosemary and I have a difference of opinion when it comes to selling candles with fake promises."

I frowned. "I don't know what that means. Can you elaborate?"

Dana crossed her arms over her chest and jutted out a hip. "Why not ask her? Why ask me?"

I mimicked her position. "Because earlier this morning, Rosemary Redman's body was discovered. She's dead."

Dana's eyes went wide as she dropped her crossed arms. "Good grief? Really?" She took a step back and glanced around her room. "Wow. I didn't see that coming."

"Now you know why my partner and I need to ask you some questions," I said. "Can you tell me why you two were arguing yesterday inside her candle shop?"

Dana motioned for us to sit on the chaise while she sat across from us in the club chair. "I didn't think it was right for Rosemary to sell products with false promises. She claimed the candles she sold helped with therapeutic healing. But here's the thing—she can't say that for a fact. She's not a holistic healer of any kind."

"So you went to have words with her?" Zoie mused.

"Yes."

"Were you seeing Rosemary as a client?" I asked.

Dana stared at me for a moment before responding. "Yes, but I can't tell you much more than that."

"Figures," Needles said. *"If you need help to loosen her tongue, I have two quills that'll get the job done, Princess."*

I leaned forward in the chaise. "So you won't tell me why Rosemary came to see you for life coaching?"

"I can tell you two things. One, she was stressed about her job. Her company was a big responsibility, and she's pretty popular around this island. That hasn't always gone over well with other candlemakers."

"Anyone specific?" Zoie asked.

Dana pressed her lips into a thin line. "I can name a couple different shop owners. Believe it or not, candle making can be competitive."

"Can you tell us the names of those shops?" Zoie repeated.

"I'd have to look in my notes."

The way she said it, I got the impression that even if they *were* in her notes, she wouldn't tell us.

Time to move on.

"That was one reason," I said. "What was the second reason Rosemary was seeing you?"

Dana leaned back in the chair and crossed her legs. "Rosemary was trying to reconcile with her sister, but it was a struggle. The two women have been estranged for a while."

"Amber?" Zoie asked.

Dana nodded. "Yes."

"Why were they estranged?" I asked.

Dana shook her head. "I don't feel comfortable telling you that. Why don't you ask Amber?"

Needles zipped down from the ceiling and landed on my shoulder, his wings glowing orange and red. *"Just say the word, Princess."*

Dana's eyes went wide as she took in Needles, but she didn't acknowledge him.

"I *could* ask Amber," I said, "but she could lie, and we wouldn't know the truth."

Dana sighed. "Fine. I guess since Rosemary is dead, it wouldn't hurt to say. Amber claimed Rosemary stole family recipes their grandmother had passed down to both of them." She waved her hands in the air. "I should tell you the two sisters used to have a candle store. I can't remember what state they lived in, but it was in a supernatural town. When the store folded, Rosemary stole the grimoire filled with recipes passed down from their grandmother. Amber wanted it back, so she came to Enchanted Island to confront Rosemary. As you can imagine, this was a pretty big trigger for Rosemary. She was already seeing me because she was dealing with emotions about being...despised is a strong word, so let's just say she was highly disliked by some."

"Rosemary was highly disliked?" Zoie mused.

Dana nodded. "Oh, yeah."

"Again," I said, "anyone in particular who disliked her?"

At that moment, there was a knock on the door, and Dana stood. "Give me just one second, please."

She hurried over to the front door and yanked it open. I

couldn't hear what she said to the woman standing outside, but a few seconds later, she shut the door and hurried back over to us. "I told my 1:30 I needed a few more minutes. Can we please hurry this along?"

"Of course," I said. "Who specifically disliked Rosemary?"

"I know of a couple people. The most vocal is a mother-daughter candle-making team."

"Names?" Zoie asked.

"Alice and Faye Ashton."

"The second time we've heard about them," Needles said.

"Thank you," I said. "Just one more question. Can you tell me where you were last night from 5:00 until this morning?"

It didn't take a therapist to see Dana was trying to get a handle on her emotions. She was failing miserably, if the flush on her neck was any indication.

"That's a long time to account for. Let's see. I closed my practice here around four o'clock yesterday. I ran some errands—went to the post office, grocery store, that kind of thing." She lifted her hand to the ceiling. "I live upstairs. After my errands, I came home. I made dinner, and since I had some leftovers, I brought them to my neighbor, Miss Lotus. She's an elderly witch who doesn't always care for herself like she should."

"What time was that?" I asked.

"I'm not sure. Maybe around 7:15? I made lasagna, so that takes about an hour to prepare and cook. So, yeah, probably 7:15. Anyway, after I dropped off the lasagna with Miss Lotus and we chatted for a few minutes, I went back to my apartment and read for a while. I think I turned in around 9:00."

"Do you live alone?" Zoie asked.

Dana smirked. "Yes. Well, I have a cat, but she doesn't talk much."

Little did she know, I could communicate with plants and

animals. I was about to suggest I have a little chat with the furball, when Dana stood.

"I really must insist we wrap this up. My 1:30 is waiting for me."

I stood, and Zoie followed suit. "Of course."

Zoie reached inside her crossbody satchel and produced a business card. "Here's our card. Feel free to call if you think of anything else we might need to know."

13

According to the app, Alice and Faye Ashton lived and worked on the south side of the island, about five miles from GiGi's houseboat. When I got to the turnoff, I made a right onto Mist Holler and followed the road for about half a mile. I passed a handful of houses, but no shops of any sort. It seemed an odd location for a candle store.

"That was Dad," Zoie said as she slid her phone inside her pants. "He said not to worry, he already called GiGi and let her know you guys couldn't come for dinner tonight. He said she was put out, but when he told her what was going on, she was appeased."

I scoffed. "Of course she was. All GiGi needs is some gossip to make her happy."

When Needles didn't say anything, I looked in my rearview mirror to see why he was so quiet. Nothing he loved more than to poke the GiGi bear. But the tiny porcupine had fallen asleep with a pretzel rod stuck in his mouth.

A narrow dirt path with a Flicker & Flame sign appeared a

few feet ahead. Turning right, I drove about ten yards before I saw the Ashton property. The candle shop sat in front of their house, so instead of continuing up the gravel drive to their home, I turned left and pulled into the small parking area to the side of the store.

"We're here, Needles," I said. "You staying here or coming in?"

Needles jerked awake, nearly choking on his pretzel rod. *"Of course I'm coming in, Princess. Why would I stay out here?"*

"To continue with your nap," I said, knowing that would get his goat.

"I wasn't sleeping! I was just thinking about the case. It helps if I close my eyes."

Zoie grinned over at me as she shut her door. "That's exactly what I told Shayla, Needles."

I snorted and waited until Needles settled on my shoulder before striding to the store.

The shop was a single-story building painted a soft, buttery yellow. Large windows dominated the front of the store, and a hand-painted wooden sign proudly displayed Flicker & Flame above the door.

"Did you notice the garden and beehive area out back?" Zoie whispered as I pulled open the door and a tinkling of bells sounded.

"Sure did."

The first thing that hit me when I walked inside was the smell—lavender and sage. The same smell that permeated Dominic's ice cream truck.

"I recognize that smell," Zoie whispered.

The second thing to hit me was that this store was vastly different from Rosemary's store. Wicked Wicks had colorful candles in dozens of shapes and sizes. This store had basic, every day candles mostly in deep yellow-orange. Very few colorants.

And though it wasn't large…it was packed. So full, in fact, it was hard to walk around. Hand-woven baskets sat near the front of the store for customers to use when selecting merchandise.

A twenty-something fairy with choppy reddish-blonde hair was off to the side, standing in front of a wooden bookshelf packed with candles. She was holding a camera above her head, smiling and talking.

"Don't forget, we have Mom's signature scent on sale all this week," she said, smirking at the camera. "Perfect for these back-to-school nights when you've put the kids down, have your glass of wine, and are ready to relax. Come on down to Flicker & Flame! We've got you covered for all your relaxation needs." She made a kissy face into the camera and waved goodbye.

"Can I help you?" a woman's voice asked.

Zoie and I turned to greet the woman who walked out from the back of the store and headed our way. She had short, choppy hair the same color as the girl with the phone, and their eyes and nose were the same as well.

"Alice Ashton?" I mused, taking a chance.

"Yes? Can I help you?" she asked, looking over at the younger girl. "Faye, that's enough. Put that phone down and finish stocking the shelves."

Faye rolled her eyes and dropped her phone down onto one of the shelves. "Mother, I'm just trying to drum up business. We haven't had one customer all day."

"My name is Agent Loci-Stone, and this is Detective Stone. The porcupine flying around smelling your lovely candles is Needles. We'd like to ask you some questions."

Needles sneezed so hard he almost knocked over a candle. *"That's not a good smell, Princess."*

"Please do not knock over the merchandise," Alice said. "The policy around here is you break it, you buy it."

"What if I melt it with my smoldering gaze?" Needles mused.

"We'll keep that in mind," I said to Alice. "I have to say, the smell in here is quite lovely."

Alice gave me a tight smile. "That's my signature scent. I created it from my garden out back—lavender and sage. The scent comes in both a candle and essential oil."

"It's definitely distinctive," Zoie said.

Distinctive enough the two of us recognized the smell immediately when we walked inside the store.

"Faye!" Alice called out. "Come over here. Have you done something that the police need to be at our place of business?"

Faye scowled and hurried over to us. "No! Why would you assume they're here for me? Maybe they're here for you."

"We're here for both of you," I said.

Faye came to a stop next to Zoie and nodded at both of us. "Hello. Not sure why you're here, but I haven't done anything wrong."

"We're here about Rosemary Redman," I said. "Do you know her? And have you heard what's happened?"

Mother and daughter exchanged looks.

"We know her," Alice said. "As far as what's happened, no. My daughter and I have been here all day. Store hours are 8:00 to 5:00, Monday through Saturday. No exceptions."

Faye rolled her eyes. "Which should be against the law. Nobody should have to put in that many hours."

Alice narrowed her eyes at her daughter, but didn't say anything else.

"Earlier this morning," I said before the two women could start arguing again, "Rosemary Redman's body was found. She'd been stabbed with what appears to be a wick dipper." I glanced around the store, and my eyes settled on the display of candle-making accessories. "Sort of like the one you have hanging right there on your pegboard."

Alice sucked in a breath. "If you're implying that me or my daughter killed Rosemary, you're way off base, lady."

Needles zipped over from one of the shelves, a quill held tightly in his paw. He stopped about three inches in front of Alice's face. *"She's not a lady, she's a princess!"*

I almost snorted aloud at that.

"My partner doesn't appreciate your tone," I said. "I'm simply telling you what has happened. I did not accuse you or your daughter of anything."

I waited until Needles settled onto my shoulder before continuing. "Did either of you know Rosemary was dead?"

Both women shook their heads.

"But you knew who she was, right?" Zoie asked.

"Of course we did," Alice snapped.

"She was a candlemaker like you?" Zoie said.

Alice straightened and crossed her arms over her chest. "I am not a candlemaker, young lady." She pressed her fingertips to her chest. "I am a chandler."

Faye rolled her eyes. "Seriously, Mom?"

"I come from a long line of chandlers. We do *not* simply make candles. This isn't a hobby—this is our livelihood. My mother was a chandler, her mother was a chandler, and on it goes for three more generations."

"What is a chandler?" Zoie asked.

Alice lifted her chin before replying. "I am a maker of wax candles, something that has been around for thousands of years. A chandler is short for chandelier, as in that which gives off light. Before electricity, people used candles to light their way." She rested a hand on her chest. "I believe in the old ways. I am a traditionalist when it comes to making candles." She gestured around the room. "As you can see from my candles. All are natural with no harsh colorants or scents." She pursed her lips. "Unlike Rosemary Redman."

"So she's a candlemaker?" Needles snickered.

"Is that why you didn't like her?" Zoie asked.

Alice narrowed her eyes. "I didn't like her because she didn't adhere to tradition. I saw hints of it now and then from her candles. It's obvious someone in her family supplied her with the appropriate way to create candles, but she was rogue. She gave chandlers a bad name."

"Is she for real?" Needles asked. *"Because I kind of get crazy vibes about her. How about you all?"*

I pressed my lips together to keep from smiling. "I found some rather threatening letters sent to Rosemary from you, Alice. Care to explain?"

"Oh, Mom!" Faye whined. "Why would you do that?"

"I simply told her the truth."

I turned to Faye. "What about you? Did you not like her because she's not a traditionalist?"

Faye glanced nervously at her mom before shaking her head. "I liked Rosemary. Sort of." She lifted her hands in the air and shrugged. "And I'm a bit of a rebel myself. I don't use beeswax. I like to use soy candles."

Alice huffed. "Even my daughter is going and bucking tradition. Our ancestors would be ashamed."

"Whatever, Mom."

I thought back to Rosemary's phone yesterday morning and seeing Faye's post pop up on her Witchagram page. "I see you and Rosemary both like to make...what do they call those things you do? Posts? Videos?"

Faye's eyes lit up. "I'm technically a candlemaker *and* a

Witchagram influencer. I make sure to post at least three times a day. Sometimes my videos showcasing the store. Sometimes it's just silly skits using the candles as props." She leaned in close. "I've gone viral a couple times! Do you follow me on Witchagram? Is that how you know what I do?"

I nodded. "Something like that."

"I love Witchagram," Zoie said. "I'm not sure if I'm following you. I'll have to check and see."

Faye beamed. "That would be great. I have quite a number of followers. I wish Mom would learn to embrace Witchagram. If given a chance, I could be just as popular as Rosemary." As if realizing what she'd just said, she held up a hand. "That probably wasn't the best thing to say. But I feel like we're losing money to Rosemary because she's so cool in her videos. So, I've spent a lot of time trying to do what she does." She gave her mom a stern look. "Not that Mom appreciates the help for our store."

"Making a fool of yourself on camera," Alice said through clenched teeth, "is *not* how you sell candles."

"Let's get back to Rosemary's murder," I said. "The store sells mostly beeswax candles here?"

Alice nodded. "That's right. We make our own candles right here on the premises. I have a couple large beehives out back."

I nodded. "Okay. And, Alice, where were you last night from 5:00 until you opened this morning?"

"Last night was Thursday. I left here a little early, around 4:30, so I could go home, grab a quick bite to eat, change my clothes, and make it into town for the TCPW meeting at 6:00."

"What's TCPW?" Zoie asked.

"Traditional Chandlers of the Paranormal World," Alice said. "We meet once a month on Thursdays."

Faye rolled her eyes. "Mom, it's you and two other old ladies sitting around talking about the good old days when people just bought candles instead of an entire experience."

Alice cut her eyes to her daughter before continuing. "So, I was at the TCPW meeting from 6:00 to 7:00, and then I drove around for a while, just thinking. I probably made it back home around 8:00."

"And, you, Faye?" I mused.

"It was 8:15, Mom," Faye said. "I go live at 8:00 every night to wish my candle fans a good night and just chat for a little bit. As I was getting off, you were pulling in."

I could tell Alice wasn't happy with her daughter's clarification. "Fine. I guess I got home around 8:15."

I frowned. "So, you basically spent a little over an hour just driving around and thinking?"

"Yes."

She didn't elaborate.

"This seems very suspicious to me, Princess," Needles whispered. *"The island isn't even that big."*

"And you?" Zoie asked Faye.

"I closed the shop around 5:00. I met some friends for dinner around 5:30. We ate at High Seas Bar & Grill. It's a restaurant on the south side of the island. I was home by 7:00 because I needed time to prepare my latest candle to showcase when I say goodnight to my followers." She waved a hand in the air. "Every night, I choose one of my soy candles that speaks to me and that I feel will speak to my followers. I tell them all about the candle —how it's made, the scent that was used, the colorant—all of it. They really appreciate it."

"So, you were home from 7:00 until you went to bed?" I asked.

"Yes."

I nodded. "I think that's all the questions we have for now."

Zoie pulled out two cards and handed one to each woman. "Here are our numbers. If you remember something that might be helpful to our case, we would appreciate a call."

As we exited the candle shop, I turned to Zoie. "Pull up Faye's Witchagram account, and let's see what she has going on."

A winding cobblestone path led from the shop's front door to the house at the back, flanked by carefully tended gardens filled with herbs and flowers. The house was a cozy two-story cottage with ivy creeping up its stone walls. To one side of the property stood the beekeeping area, a neatly arranged cluster of hives.

As I turned the Bronco's engine over and we headed down the dirt path, Zoie pushed play on a video.

"I don't know why Red Flame is so mad," Faye's voice rang out from the phone. "Accusing me of copying her. I use soy candles…she uses beeswax. There's a *huge* difference. So, if that wannabe wants to start trash, that's fine. I don't mind taking out the trash."

I glanced at Zoie. "That sounds like a threat to me."

Zoie nodded. "Especially since we now believe the murder took place near the trash bin behind her store."

"I was leaning toward the mom, but the daughter has clawed her way on top as the killer."

Zoie went back to scrolling on her phone. "I pulled up Rosemary Redman's Witchagram. She was Red Flame. Scrolling through Faye's posts, Rosemary wasn't wrong. Faye was copying everything Rosemary did, even some of the skits were very similar." She pushed play on another video, and this time, it was Rosemary's voice coming from the phone. "'Hey, Soy Queen. Why don't you grow up and find your own voice?'" Zoie continued to scroll. "It went back and forth for a while, but then, about three weeks ago, it looked like Rosemary stopped commenting on anything Faye put out or tried to call her out on. It was like Rosemary just disappeared."

"Three weeks, you say? About the time her sister came to the island," I said, making a right to head out to The Spellmoore. "I wonder if one doesn't have something to do with the other?"

Zoie nodded. "The last exchange, Faye pretty much tells Rosemary she better watch her back."

"Do me a favor and text Grant the names of the suspects we have so far for a background check."

14

"Done," Zoie said as she slipped her phone back inside her jeans pocket. "Grant texted he was at the station, and he'd get right on the names. Oh, and he said to tell you the biodegradable takeout box didn't have any marking to tell what restaurant it came from, but the scraps inside looked and smelled like a cheeseburger."

"Lots of restaurants on the island sell burgers," I said.

"But Pyra told us she stopped at Boo Burgers on her way home."

I nodded. "True, but that was at 5:00 on her way home. I doubt Rosemary would eat a cold or reheated burger around 7:30."

She turned in her seat to look at me. "He also said Serena went to her mom's for a while, and then took the twins home. I think he's still worried about what they experienced this morning."

The fact they knew enough to work a soothing spell on Dominic made me wonder if they hadn't somehow picked up on the *emotions* of the place. Not so much what had happened, but the feelings surrounding it. Which also made me think they might have some empath tendencies. Which made sense in a way—they were, after all, twins. They already shared an amazing connection we'd all witnessed. Why would it be a stretch to think they could also sense and read the emotions of others around them?

"*Serena is going to blame herself for a long time, Princess,*" Needles said from the backseat.

I sighed. "I know."

For a moment, I entertained the thought of taking Serena to Howling Good Time. The owner and barkeep there had a lot of fun getting Serena drunk with shots the last time we went. Of course, that was because he made Serena take a shot for every question I asked him when he was a potential suspect in a previous case.

But seeing as how I had to pretty much levitate her out of the car, and Grant had to carry her inside, that probably wouldn't be a wise thing to do two days before the twins' birthday. The older we got, the harder it was to bounce back.

"I haven't been back to The Spellmoore since Brick and I went to his senior prom," Zoie said.

I glanced out the corner of my eye at her. Rarely did she bring up Brick's name anymore, and I never mentioned him unless she did first.

"Have you heard from him lately?" I asked.

Brick graduated high school a year before Zoie, joined the Paranormal Police Academy, and then transferred to PADA to become a detective so he could partner with Zoie and Harlow. It was during that time PADA realized Brick had a penchant for undercover work. Instead of him joining Harlow and Zoie like he was supposed to, PADA had moved him to the undercover division and separated the team.

Thereby separating Zoie and Brick.

"I heard from him about a month ago," Zoie said softly. "It's painful. He absolutely loves his job, but I miss him, Shayla. With all my heart, I miss him. And I don't like him being on jobs where I'm not able to cover his back."

"He's a capable vampire-witch," Needles said, his voice unusually solemn. *"He will stay alive, and he will come back to you."*

Tears pricked my eyes at Needles' kind words, and I quickly blinked them back.

"Is he due for downtime?" I asked.

"I hope so," Zoie said. "But I probably won't know until he just shows up one day."

I turned left onto the gravel road leading to The Spellmoore. Before long, the top of the inn came into view. Five miles later, I pulled up in front of the magnificent structure that was The Spellmoore. The limestone inn was four stories high, with majestic gardens and fountains leading to a twelve-foot double door. I was about to grab hold of the handle when the door suddenly opened.

"Right this way, madam," the door said.

One of the amazing features of The Spellmoore—outside of the magic carpets—was the enchanted furniture scattered throughout the large estate.

The owner, Melody Spellmoore, was standing behind a huge granite countertop. When she looked up and saw us, she waved.

"Hey, Melody," I said as we walked up to the counter. "How've you been?"

"Booked solid most weekdays and every weekend all summer long. Can't complain."

"Glad to hear it," I said, looking around, relieved there weren't too many people loitering in the foyer. "I'm looking for someone. Amber Redman?"

Melody's features softened. "I heard. I noticed Amber crying when she came in, and when I asked if everything was okay, she told me her sister had been murdered."

I nodded. "Yes."

Melody looked at Zoie and smiled. "It's been a while since I've seen you. I hear you're now a detective with PADA."

Zoie grinned. "Yep. And when I'm not on assignment, Dad lets me help Shayla."

Melody turned her gaze to Needles. "And I hear you are also teaming up with Zoie."

Needles leaped from my shoulder and did a somersault in the air, his wings glowing purple and green. *"You heard right. I keep them all in line."*

Knowing Melody wouldn't be able to understand Needles, I simply told her, "Needles says he likes his job."

"That's pushing it, Princess," Needles joked.

"Well, I can tell you Amber is in Room 326. Just go through the hallway here to the elevators and get off on the third floor."

"Thanks, Melody."

We stepped onto the elevator and made the short ride to the third floor in silence. When the doors opened, an upholstered bench with tons of tassels came to attention from across the hall.

"Watch your step, please." His tassels shook as he spoke. "We hope you enjoy your stay at The Spellmoore."

"That's so cool," Zoie whispered.

We found Room 326, and I knocked on the door. A few seconds later, Amber Redman opened it, staring out at us. Her eyes were puffy and swollen, and her hair and clothes were disheveled.

"Detective? Or was it agent? I'm sorry, I can't remember."

"Technically, it's agent now. But I've still been known to answer to detective. You remember my colleagues, Detective Stone and Needles?"

Amber nodded. "Would you like to come in?"

I motioned for Zoie to go ahead. "Thank you. That would be great."

The Spellmoore was known for its posh rooms, and this one was no different. It may not have been a suite, but it was still just as lovely and matched the décor of The Spellmoore.

She led us down a small hallway. We passed a walk-in closet on the left, and on the right was a spacious master bathroom with marble and brass countertops and accessories. At the end of the hallway, it opened into a spacious room where a four-poster bed dominated the right half of the room, and a desk, sofa, and TV dominated the left side. A large picture window was directly in front of us, and against the far wall closest to us was an ivory armoire and a nook with a mini refrigerator, microwave, and coffee service.

"You guys can take the couch," Amber said as she folded into the desk chair.

"Does this place have an open bar?" Needles mused.

"We need to ask you some more questions," I said, ignoring Needles. "It's been brought to our attention that the reason you are here, visiting your sister, is because you believe she had stolen something from you. Is that correct?"

Amber's eyes went wide. "Well, technically, I guess. But it's not the only reason why I'm here." She sighed and looked away before making eye contact again. "Okay, it *is* a big part of why I came to Enchanted Island...at first."

"Can you elaborate?" I mused.

"Years ago, Rosemary and I had a shop called Sister Wicks.

We'd actually inherited the store from our grandmother. It was supposed to go to our mother, but we lost Mom and Dad in an accident. So, when Grandma passed, she left the store to us. We changed the store name to Sister Wicks and continued to sell Grandma's candles. She also left us her grimoire, full of spells and recipes she used for certain candles."

"Where was this store?" I asked.

"Phantom Pass," she said. "So when the store closed, unbeknownst to me, Rosemary stole the grimoire. She then left town a few days later. I had no idea where she went, and for three years, I didn't hear from her. One day, I was doom scrolling on Witchagram, and I saw one of Grandma's candles. I recognized it instantly. When I delved deeper, I realized the account belonged to Rosemary, and she had a store named Wicked Wicks on Enchanted Island. I decided to come here and get my recipes back—or at least a copy of them." She shrugged. "Technically, we had joint ownership of them." She lifted both hands in the air. "And that's what I was doing here."

"Do you have the grimoire now?" Zoie asked, although we both knew the answer to that question.

Amber shook her head. "No. That's why I was headed to the shop this morning. Rosemary and I had settled our differences days ago. In fact, she told me I could come by the candle store and get the grimoire—she had it stashed in her office." She wiped a tear from her eyes. "Do you think I can get into her office and get it?"

"Zoie and I found the grimoire," I said. "I'm afraid at this time, it's in custody." I held up my hand before she could speak. "One thing we don't do is keep magical family heirlooms like that locked up. Sheriff Stone will make that determination soon."

"What will happen to the store?" Zoie asked.

Amber shrugged. "I honestly have no idea. But that grimoire belongs to me. I'm the only one left of the Redman family now."

"Makes you wonder if she would kill for it," Needles said.

"I need to ask your alibi for last night," I said. "Where were you from 5:00 until 8:00 this morning?"

"I had dinner in town around 6:00. The Spellmoore has great food, but I like getting out and going into town. After dinner, I walked a couple blocks to this bar called Boos & Brews." She laughed softly. "I like hanging out in there."

"That's Tommy's bar," Needles said. *"That should be easy enough to check."*

"How long were you there?" Zoie asked.

Amber winced. "I'm honestly not sure. Maybe until 8:30 or 9:00? I actually hang out there a couple times a week. It's a lot of fun."

"Let's say you left the bar at 8:30 or 9:00," I said. "What did you do then?"

"I came back here to The Spellmoore. They have this new system now where you have to swipe a card after hours. No longer will the enchanted door just let you in." Amber shrugged. "I guess there had been a problem here before, and it's just a security measure."

I knew what those security measures were. Not only had there been a murder at The Spellmoore a couple years ago, but earlier this year, on New Year's, there had been another murder. I figured Melody was just doubling down on security.

I stood, and Zoie followed suit. "Thank you for talking with us, Amber. If you hear from an attorney regarding Rosemary's property or store, could you let me know?"

Amber nodded. "Of course."

15

"Is it okay if we stop by Boos & Brews real quick?" I asked Zoie. "I'm sure you want to get home and get something to eat before we go back out tonight for a stakeout."

Zoie waved her hand in the air. "Sure. I love talking with Tommy. Although, it's a Friday night, Shayla. It's not going to be a quick stop."

"I hope Tommy has some pretzels," Needles grumbled from the backseat, his wings glowing blue and gray. *"I'm about to starve back here."*

My cell rang, and Zoie reached over and put it on speaker for me. "Hey, Finn. What's up?"

"Hey, Shayla. Just wanted to let you know lab results came back positive for beeswax as the substance on the floor and on Rosemary's body. And Doc said 7:30-8:00 for TOD."

"Thanks, Finn."

Boos & Brews was located in town just a couple blocks from Serena's bakery. Tommy Trollman and I had grown up together, but he didn't become my best friend until the fateful day when he rescued me from a bunch of bullying werewolves. They'd been chasing me through town—I'd gone in with Mom and GiGi that day. Since I already got enough grief from kids because of who my dad was, I did my best to keep my head down and not bring attention to myself. So when the boys started chasing me, I ran.

Tommy had been hiding out between two buildings, and when I flew by, he stuck out his tree trunk arm and clotheslined the other boys. He then threw them around like rag dolls and told them if they ever chased me or bullied me again, he'd make them regret it.

I was never openly bullied again.

And Tommy had become my only other friend besides Serena.

I'd always had a soft spot for Tommy, so when I moved back and heard he'd taken over running a bar after someone defaulted on a loan he'd given them, I was thrilled to pick up where we'd left off.

"Well, look what the cat dragged in," Tommy called out from behind the bar when Zoie, Needles, and I strolled in.

"Hey!" a leopard shifter joked. "It wasn't me!"

I laughed and headed over to Tommy. "What are you doing behind the counter? You don't usually sling suds."

"My regular bartender called in."

"The vampire?" I mused.

Tommy grinned and passed Needles a bowl of pretzels. "Yep. His little girl started kindergarten this week, and I guess the whole experience kicked his butt. He said he and his wife are so drained, they can't move from the couch. His mother-in-law had to come over and make dinner for his daughter tonight." He waggled his eyebrows at me. "Now that I'm dating a woman with kids, I totally understand where he's coming from. I told him not to worry, he could have the entire night off to recoup."

I laughed. "Listen, I won't take up much of your time. I know it's a busy Friday night for you. I was just hoping you could confirm an alibi for me for last night. Were you working?"

"No. It's been a pretty stressful week in Pepper's household as well. First time for Caleb to attend school in town."

I knew some of Pepper's backstory. When I met her months ago, I'd found her, her son, and little girl hiding in a log. They had stumbled over a body, and then heard the killer come back. They fled and hid out until Needles and I found them, with the help of the forest trees.

I knew Pepper was running from an abusive husband—or possibly ex-husband. Unfortunately, she's not even sure, and she's too afraid to do some digging for fear her ex would find out. I knew he was a bigwig of some kind. A judge? A sheriff? The mayor of whatever small supernatural town she fled from? It was someone big enough she was afraid her name would pop if it ever went into the system.

And despite Tommy's assurances he'd never let anything happen to her or her children, she refused to let him find and take care of the ex, once and for all.

"Caleb is going to school in town?" I mused.

Tommy nodded. "I talked Pepper into it. Caleb came home loving it every day, but Pepper is still pretty protective, as you can imagine. So, I made sure to be available to drive out to her place for dinner every night. What are you looking for?"

"A time. I need to confirm an alibi."

He wiped down the counter, then motioned for me to follow him to his back office.

"Hey, what about my drink?" an elderly werewolf called from down the bar.

"Keep it down," Tommy growled. "I'll be right back."

"I'll stay here and watch for any suspicious activity while I eat my pretzels," Needles said.

Zoie and I followed Tommy to the other side of the bar and waited for him to motion us inside.

"I've got last night's receipts here. So, Thursday night—it shouldn't have been too busy." He opened his drawer and took out a large money bag. Unzipping it, he went through a stack of receipts. "Do you have a name or possible time?"

I nodded. "She thinks her first drink was around seven. Her name is Amber Redman."

Tommy's eyes widened. "Amber? Yes, she comes in here a couple nights a week. Like I said, I haven't been here this week, but I know the last couple weeks she likes to come and hang out. She usually drops by after she eats, so that actually sounds about right." He thumbed through some receipts and nodded. "Looks like she opened a tab at 7:08, and she closed the tab at 8:46."

That was a pretty solid alibi. If she was at Tommy's having a drink at 7:08, and didn't leave until a little before 9:00, and time of death was 7:30-8:00. I couldn't see how we could keep her on as a suspect much longer.

"Thanks for the info, Tommy."

Tommy stuck the bag back in the drawer and stood. "Happy to help."

"You're coming to the party Sunday, right?" Zoie asked.

"We wouldn't miss it for the world."

We trudged back to the bar, and after prying the pretzel bowl away from Needles, we went back outside.

Zoie crossed her arms over her chest. "Amber was here when Rosemary was killed."

I nodded. "Seems that way."

"I think I'll just fly home," Zoie said. "This way, you don't have to take me back to my house, and you can just go on home."

"It's like five minutes away," I said. "You don't have to fly home."

"Nah, I actually feel like flying for a while. But we're going to meet up later tonight, right?"

I nodded. "I'm going to go home, have some dinner with your dad, and then I say we meet outside Dana's office around 7:00. I want to talk to the neighbor and confirm Dana supplied her with dinner."

Zoie nodded and shifted into her gargoyle form, her voice taking on a deep, gravelly sound. "I'll be there."

As Zoie flew off into the sky, Needles and I strolled to the Bronco and headed to the castle for dinner. I had a lot to tell Alex.

16

"I love these nights when it's just you, me, and a good stakeout," Alex joked as he drew me close for a kiss.

His lips had barely touched mine before Needles piped up. *"And me! Don't forget about me."*

I couldn't help the giggle that escaped as Needles landed on my shoulder.

We had just finished dinner and were now standing in the front yard of the castle. To save time, Alex was about to shift and fly me into town.

"As if I could forget about you, Porcupine," Alex said dryly.

"Back at you, Gargoyle," Needles said, his wings glowing purple and green.

I flipped my ponytailed red hair over one shoulder so Needles could settle in close to my neck. On nights we flew into town, he usually hitched a ride on me. He was fast, but not as fast as Alex's wing span.

Alex shifted, and being careful with his talons, swept me into his arms, pulling me against his hard, stony chest. Smiling up at him, I wrapped my arms around his bulging neck.

"Let's go find a clue," I whispered.

What normally took thirty minutes to drive into town, took about ten in the air. As we hit the outskirts, I felt Alex descending. Glancing down at the street, I saw Zoie push herself off the side of a building.

"Hey, Dad," Zoie said as Alex carefully set me down and shifted back to human form.

"Baby girl." Alex kissed his daughter on the temple. "I was just telling Shayla how much I enjoy these nights when it's just the two of us. But I have to admit, it does an old man proud when his daughter's doing a stakeout with him as well."

"The disrespect you give me, Gargoyle," Needles grumbled as he popped out from underneath my ponytail, his wings glowing red and orange.

"Is Dana up there? Do you know?" I asked, wanting to stop Needles' tirade before it started.

"There's a light on, so I assume she's in," Zoie said. "But I haven't set eyes on her yet."

"I say we go around back," I said. "I assume there's a separate entrance to get into the apartments upstairs."

We headed down the alleyway between Dana's office and the neighboring building. Sure enough, in the back were individual staircases leading to the apartments above each building.

We quietly ascended the stairs to the right of Dana's apartment.

"You're sure this is the correct apartment?" Alex asked.

I shrugged. "To be honest, no. But it's a 50-50 chance. We know where Dana's apartment is, and to be honest, I didn't think to ask what building Miss Lotus lived above when questioning Dana."

But luck was with us as an elderly woman answered the door. She had silver hair, blue eyes, and a heavily wrinkled face.

"Miss Lotus?" I asked.

"Yes," she said in a warbled voice that some elderly people develop later in life. "Can I help you, dear?"

"I'm Shayla Loci-Stone, and these—"

"Oh, Gigi's granddaughter! Yes, I know all about you."

Used to that reaction from elderly witches, I pushed on. "We won't take up much of your time. We just have—"

The older witch cut me off, leaning closer to Alex. "The sheriff? The last time I had a sheriff knocking on my door, it was Sheriff Hawkins." There was a glint in her eyes as she grinned and cackled. "He'd only been sheriff for a couple years. His daddy was sheriff before that. Goodness, me…that's going back probably forty years or so. New sheriff knocked on my door and had the nerve to write me a ticket for indecent exposure! I told him his daddy never wrote me a ticket for indecent exposure when I danced naked under the full moon!"

"Well," Alex said, "I can assure you, we are not here to give you a citation."

"I like you, Sheriff," Miss Lotus said. "And don't worry, in a couple months, it'll be too cold for me to dance naked under the full moon."

"One is never too old to dance naked under the full moon!" Needles cried, leaping from my shoulder and turning a somersault, his wings glowing purple and green.

"Oh, isn't he magnificent?" she cooed.

Needles bowed in the air. *"Yes. Yes, I am."*

Zoie let out a small laugh. "You still dance naked under the full moon?"

"Of course, dear! How else do you think nightshades grow so

well?" She clapped her hands together. "Now, if you're not here to give me a citation, then why are you here?"

"I don't know if you heard about what happened to one of your neighbors down the street?" I mused. "Rosemary Redman?"

"Oh, yes. I heard. Dreadful."

"Were you home last night?" Alex asked.

"I sure was. My lovely neighbor, Dana, worries about me some. She's a dear girl. I was watching my programs on TV, thinking about getting up and making dinner, when she knocked on my door to bring me her leftovers."

"Do you know what time that would have been?" Zoie asked.

"Let's see. *The Coven Chronicles* had just started. Do you watch that program? Oh, I just love it. That Kavanaugh family gets put through the wringer week after week, but they're still standing. And that lead actor—he's pretty easy on the eyes." She waggled her eyebrows mischievously at Alex. "Reminds me a little of you, Sheriff."

Needles again leaped from my shoulder, laughing and flipping a somersault in the air. *"I think the witch has taken a fancy to the gargoyle."*

I bit back a smile. "What time does *The Coven Chronicles* come on?"

"Thursday nights at 7:00," Miss Lotus said.

I nodded. "So Dana arrived after 7:00?"

Miss Lotus' brow furrowed, and she nodded. "Yes. Maybe ten minutes into the show. But that's okay because I have a button I push that's like magic. It stops my TV right where it was, so I don't miss a thing."

"Did Dana stay long?" I asked.

The older witch shook her head. "No, not really. She knew I was watching my program. She brought me lasagna, so we took it into the kitchen. I didn't have to heat it up because it was already warm. We chatted a bit about our day. I remember I ate the dinner while watching my program."

Alex shifted and crossed his arms over his chest. "And did you see or hear anything at all the rest of the night that seemed out of the ordinary?"

"I'm afraid not," Miss Lotus said. "My vision and hearing ain't what they used to be, and I go to bed early most nights. Usually around 9:00."

"Thank you for your time," I said. "You were very helpful."

"I was? Well, glad to hear it."

"You have a good night," Alex said.

"You tell that handsome Sheriff Hawkins next time you see him that I said hello."

Alex cleared his throat and smiled. "I sure will, Miss Lotus."

We'd just descended the stairs and were snickering over Miss Lotus and Sheriff Hawkins when Dana's door opened above us and she stepped outside. Ducking out of sight, we pressed our backs against the alley wall.

"I'm going to do a camouflage spell," I whispered. "It will keep her from seeing us, but stay against the wall. If she bumps into us, the spell will be broken."

Whispering the spell that would keep us hidden, I pressed my fingertip against my lips, reminding them all to remain silent.

Dana was dressed casually in shorts, summer top, flip-flops, and a satchel purse. After she passed us, I waited a few more seconds before breaking the spell.

"Looks like she went left at the sidewalk," Alex said.

"I'll go take a look," Needles said as he zipped away.

Alex, Zoie, and I followed at a slower pace. At the end of the alleyway, we glanced left and saw Dana heading down the sidewalk toward Dominic's store and the candle shop.

"*She's on the prowl,*" Needles said as he flew back and settled on my shoulder.

"Let's go," I said. "But be sure to hang back."

"Should we glamour ourselves, just in case?" Zoie asked.

I shook my head as we headed down the sidewalk. "We should be okay as long as we stay low."

We hung back when Dana stopped in front of Wicked Wicks and knocked on the door. A few seconds later, she entered the store.

"What's going on?" Zoie asked. "The candle store should be closed."

"Guess Pyra is staying open late tonight," I murmured.

"Do we know who inherits yet?" Alex asked.

I shook my head. "Not yet."

Zoie huffed. "How are we going to see what's going on without being caught?"

"*I can go see what's going on,*" Needles said. "*They'll never see me.*"

I nodded. "Okay. Be careful and don't get caught."

"*Not in this lifetime, Princess.*"

He was gone for about two minutes before he sped back to us, his wings glowing red and purple. "*Hide! Hide! She's coming out!*"

Ducking into a nearby alleyway, the three of us pressed our backs against the building as Needles landed on my shoulder. Once again, I threw up a camouflage spell and waited for Dana to pass by.

"*I think Dana was just buying stuff. She kept picking up candles and putting them back down. She then took one to the counter and paid for it. Pyra was talking the entire time Dana shopped.*"

Dana finally passed by us carrying a bag with Wicked Wicks' logo on the front. Breaking the spell, we crept to the sidewalk and watched as Dana went back to her apartment. I was about to suggest we go inside the candle store to see what was going on… when a car door slammed in the back alley. The three of us turned and jogged to the back, but Pyra was already driving away.

"What?" Zoie mused. "Dana just *had* to buy that candle right then?"

"I don't know," I said. "But before it gets too late, let's go pay Alice and Faye a visit."

As Zoie and Alex shifted into their gargoyle forms, Needles settled under my ponytail. Lifting me in his strong arms, Alex took us to the sky.

A few minutes later, as we passed over Flicker and Flame Candle Store, I could see a light on inside the shop.

"Let's hit the house first," I said in Alex's ear.

Alex and Zoie landed in the side yard next to the beehives before shifting back into human form. There was only one light on inside the house, and it was upstairs.

"Faye told us she likes to get ready before she says goodnight to her fans around eight o'clock," I said. "So, my guess is that's her bedroom."

"You want to go see?" Zoie asked.

I nodded. "Let's go."

"I'll wait here," Alex said.

I waited for Zoie to shift before levitating myself up to the second-story window. Sure enough, Faye Ashton was putting on the last of her makeup and talking to herself in the mirror.

The window was open, and it sounded like she was rehearsing lines and what to say. Standing, she picked up the candle in front of her and started striking different poses in front of the mirror—sometimes holding the candle to her face, sometimes lowering it and just making various expressions.

"It's weird she does that," Needles said. *"I don't understand it."*

"I don't get it either," I whispered.

Faye then grabbed her phone, scrolled, and held the phone out in front of her. She repeated this a few times, muttering to herself.

"What is she doing?" Needles asked.

"I think she's looking for different filters," Zoie whispered.

"I don't think we're going to get anything from her."

We lowered ourselves to the ground just as Alex hissed for us to hurry. Running behind a tree he was standing next to, we watched as Alice exited the back of her store and hurried across her front lawn toward the beehives. I had a moment of panic. Had she seen us spying? But when she veered off and headed for the hives, I realized she was probably just checking on them.

As she got closer, she threw up a light orb to help light her way.

"How are my babies tonight?" she asked, putting her hand on the hive. "Work hard, my little bees. With Rosemary Redman out of the picture, something tells me I'm going to need you to be even more productive little bees."

She stood there a few more seconds, peering down at the hive. Turning, she waved her hand in the air, extinguishing the light orb overhead. Still talking to herself, she didn't even pause as she passed by us, not five yards away. When the front door to her house opened and closed, the three of us let out the collective breaths we'd been holding.

"That wasn't creepy at all," Zoie muttered.

"But she's not wrong," I said. "With Rosemary dead, she

probably *will* get an increase in sales. Especially since we don't know who will inherit the shop."

"How are her financials? Do you know?" Alex asked.

I shook my head. "I'm sure Grant will be able to tell us more tomorrow, but I will say, when we went into her shop today, the daughter mentioned they hadn't had one customer all day."

"Where now?" Alex asked.

"Rosemary Redman's house," I said.

17

Rosemary Redman lived on the east side of town in a small one-story cottage. Alex and Zoie landed on the grass, and Alex set me down before we headed for the front door. I wondered how difficult it would be to get inside. If Rosemary warded her place, it might take a while for me to break down that ward.

Ten minutes later, I finally opened the front door and stepped inside. It smelled a lot like her candle shop, and was neat but lived in. After searching her living room, we came up empty. Same with the kitchen—just a couple dishes in her sink and discarded mail on her counter.

Once that was cleared, we headed down the hallway.

"You take her bedroom," I said to Zoie. "Your dad and I will take the other room."

"I'll go with Miss Zoie."

The other room turned out to be her office and candle-making room. A desk was pushed up against the far wall, a filing cabinet sitting next to it. In the middle of the room was a wooden table piled high with candles and candle-making supplies—including a wick dipper.

The room smelled of sandalwood, sage, lavender, and rosemary.

"It's not an exact match," Alex said, "but that looks a lot like the murder weapon."

I nodded. "It does. You take her desk, and I'll take the filing cabinet."

I conjured gloves for Alex and myself and headed for the filing cabinet. Starting at the top, I opened the drawer and snorted. "Jackpot! There's a file with Dana Dunphrey's name on it."

Zoie and Needles strolled into the room as Alex turned to me.

"Nothing significant in her bedroom," Zoie said. "You guys find anything?"

I nodded. "Take a look at this." I waited for them to gather around me. "Looks like these are printed-out emails. The first couple just talk about Rosemary and Dana joining forces to produce a line of therapeutic healing candles. Then, a couple emails later, Rosemary sends a message saying she isn't going to go in this direction with Dana. Instead, she has something else in mind. The next couple emails are basically from Dana, and they're just rants. Dana's obviously angry."

"I'll say," Zoie said. "Her last line is, 'You stole my idea. You'll regret it!' That sounds threatening to me."

"Me too," Needles said.

"That email was a month ago," Alex said.

"So Dana didn't tell us the entire story," Zoie said.

I snorted. "I don't feel like anyone has told us the entire story in this investigation."

"Take a look at the next email," Alex said.

I scanned the page. "Looks like Rosemary no longer wanted to see Dana as a holistic life coach."

"Look down here," Zoie said. "Two emails later, Rosemary told Dana to stop contacting her, or else."

"That was two weeks ago," Alex said.

"I'm not sure if this is duplicitous or not," I said. "Dana *did* tell us she was angry because she believed Rosemary wasn't qualified to market candles that touted healing therapeutic properties. Although, that could have been enough of a catalyst for Dana to decide she needed to take Rosemary out."

"But Rosemary's been selling the candles," Zoie said. "So why take her out now? Why wait a month?"

"Good question," I said. "Maybe that's something we need to ask Dana."

"I think I have something for you," Alex said, pulling out a manila folder from the filing cabinet.

"Nice one," I said, reading the label.

It wasn't so much a paper but an envelope with the name Xavier Oakman Law Offices on the front. The envelope was opened, with nothing inside.

"Think this was a copy of her will?" Needles asked.

"If it was, it could go a long way toward motive," Zoie said.

I withdrew my phone and pulled up the number for the law office and wasn't surprised when it went to voicemail. I left a message and told Xavier to call me back as soon as possible.

"What will we do with the bees in the backyard?" Zoie asked.

I pointed to the empty envelope. "Depends on what the will says—if this is indeed the will. Hopefully, Rosemary made a plan for them."

18

"You better get me two *caramel-dipped pretzel rods today, Princess,*" Needles said as I opened the door to Enchanted Bakery and Brew. *"Something tells me it's gonna be a two-pretzel-rod day."*

I snorted. "I'll see what I can do, Needles."

It was barely after eight on Saturday, but already the bakery was packed. I stood in line behind Mr. and Mrs. Bloodthorn and did my best not to make eye contact with anyone in the room. The last thing I needed was to answer a ton of questions about Rosemary's death.

When the bell tinkled overhead, I looked over my shoulder and smiled at Dominic Chase coming in from outside.

"Hey," I said. "How you doing today?"

Dominic was dressed in a hot pink T-shirt with yellow and black checkered pants. "I'm doing better today, Shayla. Thanks for asking. Morning, Zoie."

"Hey, Dominic."

We shuffled forward, and I noticed with relief that we were almost to the display case. So far…so good.

A familiar cry went up across the room, and I smiled as Cayden and Brooke levitated themselves into the air. They were both strapped inside activity centers, which hovered about five feet off the ground.

"There's nothing right about that, Princess," Needles said from my shoulder.

Serena glanced over at the twins and shook her head before going back to waiting on customers.

"You've got the twins here," I said when I finally reached the display case.

"Mom forgot she said she'd watch them for me this morning," Serena replied. "I wanted to work a few hours before heading out to grab last-minute things for the party. When I got to her place, she wasn't there. I called her, and she'd totally forgotten and was out running her own errands. So, I brought them with me."

I pursed my lips in thought, then pointed to a muffin. "I'll take a blueberry-lemon muffin this morning with my coffee."

"I think I'm gonna do an elderberry scone with a hot chai," Zoie said.

"That sounds good," Dominic said. "I'll take the same."

I wasn't sure if the twins had just caught sight of Dominic from their vantage point, or if they heard his voice, but both of them stopped twirling mid-air, reached out their arms, and grasped at the air.

The chatter in the bakery died away as the twins slowly moved themselves across the packed room inches from everyone's heads, both of them screaming with delight.

"I can watch them for you, Serena," Dominic offered. "The only thing I was going to do this morning was make sure the van was packed with party supplies before we go out to Black Forest later on."

Serena bit her lip. "I don't know…"

Tamara strolled out of the back kitchen, three trays of goodies hovering above her head. "I've got fresh blueberry-lemon muffins, double chocolate chip cookies, and cinnamon rolls."

The twins stopped moving, hovering near us, both babbling nonsense words.

"Are you sure, Dominic?" Serena asked.

"Absolutely," he replied, grinning up at the twins. "What do you say, guys? You want to spend the morning with me?"

Cayden and Brooke giggled. "Ic!"

"Oh," Dominic said, "and Pyra texted me a few minutes ago. The ward to the office is down, so I can get the candles for you today."

"I would really appreciate that, Dominic." Serena waggled her finger at her kids. "And you two behave for Dominic."

The twins just giggled in response.

"Either his office will be trashed," Needles whispered in my ear, *"or it'll be set on fire."*

My cell phone pinged. It was Doc. The autopsy was ready.

I plunked my money on the counter and motioned for Zoie to grab the bag as I grabbed our coffees. "Gotta run. Talk later, Serena."

* * *

Since it was a Saturday, and the dragon lady, Pearl Earthly-Caraway, wasn't sitting behind her desk when Zoie and I bounded down the stairs a few minutes later, we were able to go right on back without an exchange of wits and wills.

I actually missed it.

Alex and Grant met us inside Doc's laboratory.

"Rosemary's estimated time of death was pretty accurate," Doc said. "As Finn already told you, I put it now between 7:30 and 8:00. Cause of death was exsanguination due to a wick dipper in the neck. She was relatively healthy outside of that."

"As you know," Finn said, "the substance came back as beeswax. Scents were sage and lavender."

"No fingerprints on the notes found at the scene, either," Harlow added. "But we *were* able to discover something that might be helpful."

"What's that?" Zoie asked.

"There were two types of beeswax found at the scene," Finn said. "Harlow and I have done extensive research of different types of beeswax, and we discovered one type of beeswax on Rosemary's hand was smoother and more processed, while the one with the scent was tackier, meaning it was likely more raw and unprocessed."

My pulse leaped at that. "Which makes sense. Rosemary wasn't a traditionalist. She used dyes and other elements in her beeswax. When Zoie and I went into Flicker & Flame, the Ashton's store, their candles were more yellow and natural looking."

"Exactly," Finn said. "So here's the question—why did the murder weapon have no traces of beeswax, and yet two types of beeswax are found on the body? In other words, if the killer wore gloves, how did the scented, unprocessed beeswax like Alice uses get transferred to Rosemary's skin and clothing?"

"That *is* odd," Zoie agreed.

"You think maybe the killer did it on purpose?" Alex asked.

"Like the killer was trying to frame Alice?" Grant mused.

Finn shrugged. "Hard to say. But Harlow and I thought you should be aware of the oddity."

"That's definitely a question we're going to want to find the answer to," I agreed. "Anything else?"

"Yes," Harlow said. "Sheriff, maybe you can take pity on me and total out the ice cream truck? Just tell Dominic it can't be saved?"

I laughed. "And not get to see you sell cute little popsicles to kids out of it?"

Harlow glared at me. "Never going to happen."

"I might be on Harlow's side for this one," Zoie said. "I mean, would you want your kids buying ice cream from a truck that had a dead body in it?"

"No amount of sage is going to cleanse that," Harlow said.

"Hmm." I pursed my lips. "You might be right. Let me talk with GiGi. Maybe she knows something that can help with that."

"A demolition?" Harlow asked hopefully.

Alex and Grant both chuckled.

I snorted. "And deprive all the adorable children on Enchanted Island. Not likely."

19

"I have a call into Xavier Oakman," I said as we settled down into chairs around Grant's desk. "Hopefully, I'll hear back from him soon."

"Down to two snack-sized bags of pretzel rods, Gargoyle," Needles said as he zipped into the main office. *"You trying to kill me?"*

"For years," Alex deadpanned.

I laughed. "Stop it, both of you."

"Serena put in an extra caramel-dipped pretzel stick for you, Needles," Zoie said, motioning to the open bakery box on Grant's desk.

"Guess we can save what we got for later," I said, peeking inside the box of goodies and snatching a chocolate-chip scone.

"I'm surprised she didn't tell you she gave me a box already," Grant said.

I snorted. "Well, she was pretty sidetracked, what with the twins doing their spotlight trick."

Grant groaned. "What did they do?"

I grinned and took a bite of the scone. "Levitated themselves up above everyone so they could get quick access to Dominic." I took a sip of my coffee to wash down the bite. "Now Dominic is watching the twins today until Serena finishes her errands this afternoon."

"Poor Dominic," Grant said. "That guy is a stand-up vampire. Not many twenty-somethings would joyfully hang with twins that weren't his."

"It's crazy how much they've taken to him," Zoie said. "I think it scares Harlow to see how good he is with kids."

Needles snorted. *"Should we take bets on when he's going to pop the question?"*

"Don't let Harlow hear you say that!" Zoie said. "Even joking, she'll hex you a good one."

"Okay," Alex said. "Let's hear what we have so far from PADA."

"Real quick," I said. "We know we are working with a time of death between 7:30 to 8:00."

Grant picked up the file on his desk. "I have Rosemary's sister, Amber Redman. Age, thirty-six. Single, no children. She's a chandler." Grant looked up from the file and smiled. "I had to look that up. It's a fancy name for candlemaker." He took a sip of his coffee. "She lives in a paranormal town called Phantom Pass in Ohio. No criminal history, but her business financials are dismal. Three years ago, she and Rosemary filed bankruptcy on their candle store in Phantom Pass. Other than the rent she collects from the building that was given to her and Rosemary when their grandmother died, I have no other business income showing for her. Her personal finances are a little more stable, but not by much."

"Motive?" Alex asked.

Zoie brushed crumbs from her hands. "Amber believes her

sister stabbed her in the back when she stole their family grimoire and fled Phantom Pass. For three years, Amber had no idea where Rosemary went. Then, she sees Rosemary and her candles on Witchagram. She recognized her grandmother's recipes from the candles Rosemary was selling, so she decides to come to Enchanted Island and confront her sister."

"Alibi?" Alex asked.

"It's pretty solid," I said. "We have time of death between 7:30 and 8:00, according to Doc. Well, from 7:00 to 9:00, Amber was sitting in Tommy's bar having drinks. I think at this time, we can take her off the suspect list, or at least drop her way down."

"Next up," Grant said, "Alice Ashton. Age, fifty-two. Fairy. Divorced, one adult child. Also a chandler. Alice was born and raised on Enchanted Island. She does have a criminal record. She received a misdemeanor offense for terroristic threats and unauthorized use of magic eight years ago. According to the report, she threatened to burn down another candlemaker's business if they didn't stick to traditional candle making." Grant looked up and shrugged. "Whatever that is."

"Does it say who she threatened?" I mused.

Grant ran his finger down the page. "Yes. I remember reading that earlier. Here it is. Grilla Truehart." He took a sip of his coffee. "Alice was also arrested for protesting and picketing in an unauthorized location. This happened about four years ago. Right before any of us came to the island. The arresting officer was Deputy Sparks. He gave her a citation at first, then arrested her when it got physical. She was sentenced to a weekend in our lovely jail cell and ten hours community service."

"So she's a hothead," I said. "As Zoie, Needles, and I have already seen."

"She's definitely fanatical about her candle making," Zoie agreed.

"Both her business and personal finances look okay," Grant said. "Nothing really popped out at me."

"Motive?" Alex asked.

"Alice is a—well, she's fanatical when it comes to maintaining what she believes is the 'true way' of candle making. When we visited her shop, Zoie and I noticed her candles were yellow, and very few had colorants in them. Alice stays to the 'natural' way of beeswax. And she believes in the sanctity of that preservation so much, she obviously has attacked others who don't share her beliefs." I shook my head. "She was even upset at her daughter, who has been dabbling in soy candles." I shrugged. "And I think she was jealous of Rosemary. Her daughter wanted to emulate Rosemary, *and* Rosemary's candles are big sellers on Enchanted Island."

"It wouldn't be hard to imagine Alice killing Rosemary," Zoie agreed.

"And she had opportunity," **Needles** added.

"Needles is right," I said. "Alice told us she was at a meeting in town from 6:00 to 7:00. That would give her time to grab a quick takeout dinner and make it to Wicked Wicks around the time of the meetup. She told us she drove around the island for a little over an hour and returned home around 8:15."

"That means she had opportunity," Zoie said. "So she stays on the list?"

I nodded. "She stays on the list."

"Next, I have Faye Ashton," Grant said. "Age, twenty-five. Fairy. Single, no children. Born and raised on Enchanted Island. She's also a chandler and works in her mom's store. She has no criminal record, but her personal finances are in the red. Quick scan shows she spends way more than she makes. Has a credit card debt that will take her forever to dig out from."

"Motive?" Alex asked.

"Jealousy," I said. "I feel that's the biggest thing it boils down to. Zoie found a ton of videos in which Faye and Rosemary take digs at each other. Faye mentioned more than once how if her mom would just let her do her own thing, she could be as big as Rosemary on Witchagram. To tip the scale a little more, Rosemary called out Faye numerous times on social media about how Faye needs to stop copying her and do her own thing. Which, of course, Faye sniped back at."

"Alibi?" Alex mused.

"She told us she had dinner with friends, but left around 7:00. She then went home to get ready for her nightly goodnight live session with her followers. She told us she usually takes an hour to get into the zone, pick the candle that speaks to her, practice her lines, all that. So according to her, she was home from 7:00 to 8:00 getting ready to go live at 8:00. Zoie checked her account, and she *did* go live at 8:00 from her bedroom, so that much is true."

Zoie nodded. "What we *can't* say for sure is that she didn't drive into town, which would be about twelve minutes from the restaurant where she was. Grab a bite, take it to Rosemary, kill her, stuff her body in the truck, hurry home, and go live at 8:00."

I took a sip of my coffee. "It's technically doable...just not sure it's plausible."

"Especially since it takes her so long to practice her lines," Needles said.

"So she stays on your list?" Alex mused.

I nodded. "Yes."

Grant popped a cookie in his mouth and shuffled papers. "Next, I have Dana Dunphrey. Age, thirty-three. Fairy. Single, no children. She's self-employed as a holistic life coach. She's lived on Enchanted Island for eight years. Criminal background showed a misdemeanor fine twelve years ago for practicing magic without a license. She's had one civil complaint lodged while living here. Looks like it was five years ago. Must have been settled because I don't see anything more on file. Her financials aren't the greatest. She's barely making a living as a holistic life coach."

"Motive?" Alex asked.

Zoie took a sip of her chai. "For starters, major betrayal. Dana was angry at Rosemary because Rosemary not only backed out from the tentative candle-making deal they had going on, but then Rosemary went and fired Dana from being her life coach."

"Plus," I added, "I overheard Rosemary and Dana fighting on Thursday morning. Dana was in the store, angry at Rosemary for the therapeutic candles. They had words."

Alex took a sip of his coffee, then reached inside the box for a chocolate-chip cookie. "Alibi?"

"Dana closed her office at 4:00," I said. "Ran errands, then returned home around 6:00. She made lasagna for herself and her neighbor. She ate, then took the leftovers to Miss Lotus. When we spoke to the neighbor, and she corroborated Dana came over. We put her at Miss Lotus' house from 7:10 to 7:20."

"Still giving her time to pick up takeout and run down to Wicked Wicks," Zoie pointed out.

I nodded. "True. But Dana stated she went home after dropping off the food to Miss Lotus and read until 9:00."

"So she stays on the list?" Alex asked.

I nodded. "She stays on the list."

"Last is Pyra Thornby," Grant said. "Age, twenty-three. Witch. Single, no children. Born and raised on Enchanted Island. She lists sales and chandler under occupation."

"I've checked out her Witchagram account as well," Zoie said. "She doesn't have near the following or videos as Faye Ashton or Rosemary Redman."

"Her financials are fair," Grant continued. "She lives within her means, but it's meager. Nothing too substantial on her criminal record. I arrested her last year for public trespassing, disturbing the peace, and public mischief. One of her social media recordings went a little too far, and she was given a citation." He paused and looked up. "Basically, she trespassed onto someone's property to do a video, and they pressed charges. She paid a two-hundred-dollar fine and did ten hours of community service."

"Motive?" Alex asked.

"I overheard a disagreement between Rosemary and Pyra on Thursday after Dana left the store," I said. "Rosemary told Pyra she needs to wait for her time, that it will come, but it wasn't right now. I got the feeling Pyra was pushing to do more social media videos like Rosemary did. At the end of the discussion, Rosemary asked Pyra if they were good, but Needles and I both agreed it didn't sound like Pyra had forgiven Rosemary."

"Not in the least," Needles said. *"That girl was mad."*

"Alibi?" Alex said, downing the last of his coffee.

"Rosemary closed the shop around 5:00," I said. "She told Pyra she was going to stick around for a while longer, so Pyra left. She picked up dinner and went home, watched TV, then went to bed. She has a roommate who came home a little after 11:00, so that doesn't help much with corroboration."

"So she stays on the list?" Alex asked.

I nodded. "She stays on the list."

"Where are you guys off to next?" Alex asked.

"I'd love to talk with Grilla Truehart," I said. "I want to know exactly what went down between her and Alice. The anger level there." I glanced at the clock on the wall. "And I'm hoping to hear from Xavier soon about who inherits the candle shop."

Zoie frowned. "Does it matter as much now that we know Amber has been eliminated?"

"Oh, yeah," I said. "Especially if Rosemary had a will *before* her sister came to the island. Think about it. Let's say Rosemary was training Pyra to take over for her in the event of her death. But then Amber comes to town and she and Rosemary make up. Could be Pyra killed Rosemary hoping she could kill her before she had time to change her will *or* maybe Pyra caught wind Rosemary changed her will, and in her anger, she killed Rosemary." I shrugged. "But it's a moot point until we know what's in the will."

"Since we've eliminated Amber as a suspect," Alex said. "Why don't I call her and let her know she can come pick up the grimoire?"

"That would be a help, thanks." I stood and stretched. "We'll keep you posted throughout the day."

20

The road to Grilla Truehart's home snaked through the woods, narrowing the farther we drove. I knew the area we were driving—it was near the location of the first major spell I'd seen the twins perform. The night they'd used magic to move a fallen tree from the road. They'd been about eight months old, and it had been an amazing sight to behold. It also meant Across the Bridge Trinkets, the knickknack store Tommy owned and Pepper managed, was nearby as well.

My cell phone rang, and Zoie put it on speaker. "This is Agent Loci-Stone."

"Shayla? This is Xavier Oakman. How are you?"

"Xavier! Hello. I was hoping to hear from you. I'd say I'm good, but that wouldn't be entirely true. Did you hear what happened to Rosemary Redman yesterday?"

"I did. I just got back in town late last night, so I didn't get your message until a bit ago. But I needed to do some stuff on my end before I could call. Sorry about that."

"I understand. I found an empty envelope from your firm. Did you write a will for Rosemary Redman?"

"I did. About two weeks ago."

I glanced quickly at Zoie. "You made this will up two weeks ago? Who did she leave the store to?"

"Her sister, Amber Redman. Rosemary confided in me that they'd been estranged until…" He trailed off. "Is her sister a suspect?"

I shook my head, even though he couldn't see me. "No. It's just incredible timing."

He blew out a breath. "Good. My next call is to her."

"I'm sure she'll be relieved to know. Thanks, Xavier."

"My pleasure. You and Alex take care."

I smiled. "Same to you and your family."

Zoie disconnected and set my phone back on the console. "Pyra probably isn't going to be happy."

I shrugged. "Not our concern." I turned right and slowed as the Bronco bounced down a dirt path. I could just make out the house in the distance.

"Wow," Zoie whispered, as I parked near a cluster of beehives buzzing with activity. "This is amazing."

I nodded, taking in the sight of Grilla's house. It looked like something out of a fantasy novel. Built half into the hillside, it was a cross between a cave and a hobbit house, with a rounded stone doorframe and small circular windows scattered across the front. Moss crept up the edges of the thatched roof, and wildflowers were scattered everywhere I looked. A wooden sign near the path read, "Truehart Apiary and Candles."

"Apiary?" Zoie mused.

I grinned. "Beehive. She's a beekeeper."

"Why didn't she just say that?" Needles asked.

Zoie laughed. "Well, I may not know her words, but I like her style."

Grilla Truehart opened the door as we approached, her wild topknot of hair almost as untamed as the landscape around her. She was younger than I'd expected—mid-forties, like me—with sharp green eyes that flicked between Zoie and me. Something about her seemed familiar, though I couldn't quite place it.

"You're Shayla Loci, aren't you?" she mused.

I smiled. "It's Loci-Stone now."

She nodded and smiled as well. "Of course. I remember hearing you married the sheriff. You probably don't remember me. We both kept to ourselves when we were young. We were both…outsiders."

I honestly couldn't recall who she was, but I smiled anyway. "It's been a long time."

"Yes, it has."

"These are my partners, Detective Stone and Needles."

She smiled and nodded at Zoie, then waved at Needles perched on my shoulder before turning back at me. "What can I do for you, Shayla?"

"I'd like to ask you some questions about what happened between you and Alice Ashton."

Grilla shuddered. "She has a mean streak." She stepped back and motioned us inside. "Please, come in."

The inside was just as earthy and cozy as the outside.

"I like your place," Zoie said.

Grilla smiled, a hint of pride lighting up her face. "Generational, like most on Enchanted Island. My great-great-grandfather built it, and it's been passed down ever since. I've made a few updates, but it's mostly the same."

As we settled in the comfy sitting area, I wasted no time. "So about Alice Ashton?"

Grilla shook her head. "Not a stable woman."

Zoie leaned forward. "We know she was arrested for threatening you. Can you tell us about that?"

Grilla's brow furrowed, and she glanced toward the window as if gathering her thoughts. "Does this have to do with Rosemary Redman's death? My aunt lives in town, and she told me about the murder yesterday."

"Did you know Rosemary?" I asked.

"Only by reputation. I don't get out much. I make candles and honey, and I sell them in a nearby store."

"Across the Bridge Trinkets?" I mused.

Grilla's eyes widened. "Yes."

"I know Tommy and Pepper well," I said. "So about Alice?"

She sighed, brushing a strand of hair from her face. "It's been a while now. I don't do festivals anymore, but back then, I'd sometimes get a booth. The year this happened, I had one at the July Jubilation. My booth wasn't too far from Alice's table. I'm not like my mother or grandmother or great-grandmother—I don't hold to strict traditions of candle making. I love whimsy. I use both natural and artificial scents, sometimes paraffin wax instead of beeswax. Whatever works for the candle." She grimaced. "And honestly, my customers don't care. Most of them don't even realize. I tried duplicating some of the natural scents, but I just don't have that kind of magic."

"And Alice accosted you over it?" Zoie asked.

"Yes," Grilla said bitterly. "It was after the festival, and I'd done well—nearly sold out. She marched down to my booth, much to her daughter's dismay—poor girl—and used magic to scorch the last of my candles right there. Nothing but a huge pile of melted wax on the ground. She made some serious threats, but the sheriff showed up before it went further."

"Is that why you stopped doing festivals?" I asked.

She nodded. "It just wasn't worth it. I do good business selling at Across the Bridge Trinkets. That's enough for me."

"Do you think Alice has a temper?" Zoie asked. "Enough to harm someone?"

Grilla hesitated, then sighed. "The day she attacked me and my candles, she was completely out of her mind. Tunnel vision. No matter what I said, it didn't matter. She considered me a threat, and she was going to eliminate that threat."

21

It was nearing 12:30 when I parked the Bronco in front of Dana's office. I remembered she told us she usually took her lunch from 12:30 to 1:30, so I hoped we hadn't missed her.

As luck would have it, Dana was locking her front door when Zoie, Needles, and I exited the vehicle. She started when she turned around and saw us.

"Oh, hello. I was just on my way out for lunch." She held up the brown paper bag and gave it a shake. "Was heading to the park."

"Our questions won't take long," I said.

She couldn't hide the flash of irritation that crossed her face. "Of course. How can I help you?"

"We'd like some clarification regarding emails between you and Rosemary. Specifically, the ones where you and Rosemary converse about collaborating on a project regarding healing therapeutic candles."

Dana's eyes widened. "You know about those?"

"We do," Zoie said.

"We also know Rosemary later retracted her agreement to partner with you, and shortly thereafter launched her own line of healing therapeutic candles."

Tears sprang to Dana's eyes, and she shook her head. "I couldn't believe she did that to me! I mean, I thought we were more than just client and life coach. We shared a passion for candles and helping people." A tear slipped down her cheek. "But in the end, I think it all boiled down to money. Rosemary wanted it all for herself."

"And then, she went in for the kill," I said. "She told you she wasn't going to see you as her life coach anymore."

"Yes! So you can understand why I was so mad. I'm sure those emails sounded terrible, but I was devastated. It was like she gutted me. For what? Money? Again, we were supposed to be doing the candles to help people."

"You pretty much told her she would regret doing what she'd done. You understand how we see that as a threat, right?"

Fury flashed in Dana's eyes. "I didn't mean I was going to kill her! I meant I was going to see a lawyer. She'd regret it because I was going to sue her." She swiped at the tear and glared at me. "I tried to hire Xavier Oakman, but when I told him who I wanted to sue, he told me he couldn't represent me because it would be a conflict of interest!" She let out a strangled cry. "Not that it matters now."

* * *

"What do you think?" I asked as we watched Dana hurry down the sidewalk toward the park, the opposite direction from Wicked Wicks.

"She definitely seems distraught," Zoie said.

I nodded in agreement. "What do you say we kill two birds with one stone? Dominic's shop is just down the street, and it's almost lunchtime. Let's go check in on Dominic and the twins, and then grab some lunch. How does that sound?"

"It sounds like you're my favorite today, Princess," Needles said, doing a flip in the air.

There were a lot of people walking the sidewalks, which wasn't a surprise for a Saturday afternoon. Zoie and I stopped a couple times along the way, people wanting to make small talk and ask about the investigation.

Before long, though, we passed by Wicked Wicks and made a beeline for Magical Events.

"Hey, did that say they were closed?" Zoie mused as she stopped and took a couple steps backward until she was in front of Wicked Wicks' door. She reached out and pushed, but it was locked. "That's weird. It's a Saturday afternoon."

I shrugged. "Maybe Amber told Pyra she was the new owner and asked Pyra to close down until she could figure out what to do next."

"You think that's what happened?" Zoie asked as she stepped inside Magical Events. "The new owner told Pyra to shut down the store?"

"Could be. Or maybe—"

The twins' squeals interrupted me, and Dominic looked up from his position on the floor and waved. "Come on in, guys. We're playing hide-the-bottle."

"Is it a bottle of rum?" Needles mused. *"Because I could use a drink."*

"What's hide-the-bottle?" Zoie asked.

The twins levitated themselves into the air, babbling and waving their hands.

"Well, I hide my eyes, and the twins do their magic thing and hide their bottles somewhere in the office, and then I go and find them."

"Oh, yes," Needles said. "That sounds totally reasonable for one-year-olds to play."

"That doesn't freak you out?" Zoie asked.

Dominic shrugged. "Nah. I think it's super cool what these baby werewitches can do." He lifted both hands fisted in the air, and the twins lowered themselves just enough to give him baby fist bumps.

Zoie and I walked over and sat next to him on the blanket on the floor.

"I noticed the candle shop was closed next door," I said.

"Yeah. Pyra texted me about an hour ago, when the twins and I were at the park. She said something important came up, and she was closing the shop for the day. She was totally cool, though, and reminded me about getting the candle for the twins out of the back office. She said she left a key for me next to Wicked Wicks' back door underneath the tin can."

"Why didn't she just leave it on the doorstep here?" Zoie asked.

Dominic shrugged. "Maybe she was afraid it would melt in the sunlight. I have no idea, but I figured I'd go over in a little bit, after I feed the twins some lunch."

Brooke handed me a Cheerio covered in baby slobber. "Num num."

I smiled and shook my head. "Better not, Brooke. Zoie, Needles, and I are getting ready to have our own lunch." I pushed the slobbery fist back at her. "You eat up."

Totally unaffected by my response, Brooke shoved the Cheerio into her mouth and giggled. I stood and waited for Zoie to stand as well. We said goodbye and headed outside.

"You guys just want to hit the sub shop down the street?" I asked.

Zoie nodded. "Sounds good to me."

"I wouldn't say no to some salty ham," Needles said.

22

"This extra-salty ham sandwich is going to hit the spot, Princess," Needles said as he vibrated on my shoulder.

Zoie and I placed our orders, and as I went to pay, I noticed Alice Ashton eating alone at a two-person table.

Zoie followed my gaze, her eyes wide. "I can't believe Alice is here."

"I can't either." While I knew everyone deserved a day off, it just seemed odd when she was so adamant that her store be open six days a week.

I paid for our lunch and grabbed the tray. Not one to pass up an opportunity, I made sure we walked by Alice's booth.

"Oh, hey, Alice," I said, doing my best to act surprised. "I didn't expect to run into you here in town on a Saturday."

Alice scowled up at us. "I had an errand to run that couldn't wait."

When she didn't elaborate, I nodded and walked to an empty booth two tables down. Zoie and I busied ourselves unwrapping the sandwiches, pushing our straws into our sodas, and making small talk. I was almost finished with my sandwich when Alice stood and threw away her trash and hurried out the door.

"Do you think it's just coincidental she's near the candle store?" Zoie asked.

I shrugged. "Probably. I can't see why she'd go into Rosemary's store. Especially now that she's gone."

"Return to the scene of the crime?" Needles suggested as he shoved a piece of ham inside his mouth.

"Maybe Dana is her life coach," Zoie said with a giggle. "And Saturdays are their meeting days."

I smiled at that. "I doubt it."

Needles belched and patted his tummy. *"That hit the spot, Princess. You're the best."*

Zoie and I wadded up our wrappers, grabbed our empty sodas, and headed for the trash receptacle. We'd just stepped outside when two things happened at once—sirens rent the air, and people down the street near Dominic's store started screaming.

"What the—"

I broke off when glass shattered and flames shot out the front window of a storefront two blocks down the street, suspiciously close to Dominic's store! My heart lurched. The twins! If that fire was anywhere near Dominic's store, they'd all be in trouble!

Needles shot off ahead of us, as Zoie and I took off running, dodging around supernaturals on the sidewalk, gawking at the scene.

"Cut to the street!" I called out. "We can go faster that way."

Zoie could have shifted, but the truth was, we were just as quick dashing down the road the short distance. I heard someone shout there were people inside the store, and I knew it wasn't good news when Needles came speeding our way, his wings glowing red and orange.

"I can't explain it, Princess!"

"What is it?" I demanded…only to have my heart drop when I realized the shattered glass was from Wicked Wicks!

A firetruck came screeching past us…but what really took my breath away was the huge gray werewolf sprinting full tilt behind it.

Grant!

Alex descended from the sky and landed next to us as Grant shifted back to human form.

"It's okay, Werewolf," Needles said. *"The twins are fine!"*

"Dominic said they were trapped inside!" Grant shouted as he pushed his way past the firemen leaping off the truck.

"No!" Needles shouted. *"That's what I'm trying to tell you, boy! It's okay. I wouldn't be out here if those babies were still inside."*

Alex, Zoie, and I ran after Grant. But I was with Grant…until we had those precious babies in hand, nothing was keeping us out of that building!

The first thing I was aware of was the relieved laughter coming from the firemen. When I finally made it to the broken-out window, I couldn't believe my eyes!

Inside the candle shop, Brooke and Cayden were hovered near the ceiling, laughing and jabbering…and making it snow! A bewildered Dominic stood frozen in the center of the shop, his pale skin looking even whiter than usual.

"Brooke! Cayden!" Grant shouted as he hurried inside the store. "Get down from there right now, before you fall!"

"Yes, that's the big takeaway here. Not the fact they just put out a fire by making it snow."

I couldn't stop the hysterical laughter that bubbled out of me. I wasn't usually frazzled by much, but of all the scenes that flashed through my mind, this never came up.

DEADLY FLAME

"Da! Da!" Brooke shouted right before she dropped to the ground...and shifted into a werewolf.

Not to be outdone, Cayden dropped and shifted as well. The two pups immediately started playing in the snow, kicking the white stuff up with their paws.

"You okay?" I asked Dominic as Alex, Zoie, and I stepped inside.

"I don't know," he said in a shaky voice. "One minute, the twins and I were in the back office picking up the candles Rosemary made...and the next thing I know, a small explosion happened, and I smelled—well, I smelled a lot of burning wax and good smells. But I knew that shouldn't be right. So I dropped the candles and—" He broke off looking a little sheepish. "And I grabbed the twins. They were in the air looking around the office. Anyway, I grabbed them and we ran out of the room, only to come face-to-face with a huge fire! My phone was in my pocket, but I had a twin on each hip. Before I could figure out what to do, they just—" He threw his hands up in the air. "They just *shot* out of my arms and started floating around, waving their hands in the air. I called the emergency number and told them what was going on, and by the time I got off, the twins were making it snow! Snow!" He glanced down at them, now horse playing and rolling around in the snow, pretending to bite each other in their werewolf forms. "They saved our lives."

"What's going on! Let me through!"

"Serena!" Grant shouted, running toward her.

"Oh, my goddess! Where are my babies! Where are my babies!"

"It's okay, Serena," Grant said, wrapping his arms around her. "They're okay."

"Where are they? I got a call from dispatch saying the twins were inside a burning building at the candle store!"

"It's okay," Grant soothed. "See, that's them playing in the snow."

It took a few seconds for Serena's mind to comprehend what she was seeing—not a blazing inferno like she was prepared to see…but her twins rolling around in snow as baby werewolves.

Her knees buckled, and Grant caught her before she hit the ground.

"Sheriff," the fire chief called out. "You might want to take a look at this."

"I'll stay here with Grant and Serena," Needles said, his wings throwing off so much color, I was almost tempted to put on my sunglasses. He was obviously distraught and having a hard time controlling his emotions.

Alex, Zoie, and I plowed our way through the mounds of snow to stand by the chief. He held a melted candle in his gloved hand.

"Being part witch and part werewolf," the fire chief said, "I have a pretty good sense of smell. And my sniffer tells me this candle is teeming with magic. Not like the others in the store. Serious magic. Plus, it's the only candle fully melted."

Alex nodded. "Go ahead and bag it for me. I'll take it to Finn for processing."

"*How* did this happen?" I demanded. "That's what I want to know. When Zoie and I came by earlier, the shop was closed and locked up tight. With all the people outside, no way someone slipped in the front door and set a fire."

"Could be a delayed spell," the chief suggested. "Maybe the candle was spelled to go off at a certain time. Could be the person who made the spell had no idea who would be in the store. They were just wanting to start a fire."

Alex cut his eyes to me. "You need us? Or are you and Zoie okay?"

"Zoie and I can handle this," I said tightly. "I got three people in mind I want to talk with. We *will* get this wrapped up today."

Alex nodded once, a muscle jumping in his jaw. "Okay."

"Who'd have thought?" Serena said with a shaky laugh as she headed our way. "I guess setting them down in front of Paraflix so much was a good thing."

I smiled at my cousin. Her color was almost back to normal. "What's that?"

She motioned around the room. "The twins have been infatuated with that children's movie *Snowbound Siblings*. It's on Paraflix. They probably watch it two or three times a day."

Paraflix was the supernatural equivalent of Netflix for humans, but I'd never heard of *Snowbound Siblings*. But, then again, I didn't have kids.

"I'm so sorry, Serena," Dominic said. "You left the care of those babies with me, and I nearly got—"

"No," Grant and Serena said simultaneously.

"You couldn't have known this would happen, Dominic," Serena said. "The only person to blame is the person who tried to burn this place down."

"With my pups inside," Grant growled, his eyes glowing yellow.

"I don't mean to freak everyone out," Needles said as he drifted down from the ceiling, *"but is that snowman over there building himself?"*

We all turned to where Needles pointed.

Sure enough, a medium-sized snowball began rolling across the ground, gathering snow until it formed a perfectly smooth sphere. With a sudden bounce, it leaped onto a larger ball of snow that had already settled in place. A smaller snowball hopped up onto the medium one, completing the snowman's body. Out of nowhere, two decorative gemstones of different colors shot off a nearby table, landing with a satisfying plop in the snowman's face.

But it didn't stop there. Suddenly, dozens of differently shaped snowballs were being formed, and in the blink of an eye, an army of snowmen stood before us, ready to take on the world.

"Cayden! Brooke!" Serena admonished. "Shift back this instant, and stop using magic to build snowmen!"

23

"Even though I'm pretty sure Pyra Thornby is behind this," I said as Zoie, Needles, and I huddled behind the fire truck five minutes later, "I still want to check in with Dana, since we are right here."

"What about Alice?" Zoie asked. "We saw her a few minutes before the building caught fire, and she pretty much did the same thing to Grilla years ago. That screams red flag to me, Shayla."

I closed my eyes and thought about that for a second. She wasn't wrong…but my gut was saying no. I opened my eyes and shook my head. "Normally, I'd agree, Zoie. But think about it. How would she have gotten the enchanted candle inside the store without Dominic or the twins either seeing or hearing her?"

"What are you saying, Princess?" Needles asked.

"I think it has to be Pyra. I'd bet anything Alice has never even stepped foot inside Wicked Wicks. It's not 'traditional' enough for her, and she's jealous. There's no way she could have placed the candle in the store. Pyra has access anytime she wants."

Zoie nodded. "You're right. I guess I hadn't thought of that."

"C'mon," I said. "Let's go check on Dana real quick before we go find Pyra."

We hurried down the street to Dana's office. It was a little after 1:30, so I figured she should be back from lunch by now. Sure enough, she was sitting behind her desk when I barreled inside, a candle burning on her desk.

"What is it now?" she asked wearily, standing. "I just answered your questions an hour ago."

"Where have you been this last hour?" I asked.

She threw her hands in the air. "You know where. I told you I was going to the park. Heck, you probably saw me go that way. Why are you asking?"

"Did you speak to anyone?" I asked.

"No. I just sat on the bench and ate my sandwich, and then came back here." She frowned. "Does this have something to do with the firetruck at the end of the street? I saw it on my way back to the office."

I stared at her, trying to figure out if she was telling the truth or not. I didn't have time to chase down citizens in the park to see if they saw Dana this past hour. The shadows from the wick played over her face, and I glanced down at the flame inside the candle. It went from bright red to a dull yellow back to bright red, and I could have sworn the flame grew and shrank as well.

Before I could ask another question, there was a knock on the door, and then the sound of someone coming inside.

"I'm sorry I'm late," a woman panted as she hurried over to us. "The street has been blocked off, and so I had to park..." she trailed off when she noticed all of us standing in the room. "Oh, I'm sorry. I didn't realize you had someone here, Dana."

"It's fine," I assure her. "We were just leaving."

I nodded once to Dana before heading back outside.

"I don't think she planted the candle over lunch," Zoie said. "Like Alice, how would she have gotten in without Dominic or the twins knowing?"

We made a dash for the Bronco and hopped inside. After looking up Pyra's home address on my interactive app, I pulled onto the street and turned to Zoie as she handed Needles a pretzel rod. "Do me a favor. Go on Witchagram and see if Pyra has posted anything recently."

Zoie yanked out her phone, and a few seconds later, she held up her phone for me to see. "Yep. She posted a video about two hours ago." She pushed play, and Pyra's excited voice filled the Bronco.

"Hey, candle lovers! This is your girl, Pyra. Coming to you from my kitchen today. Guess what?" She leaned in closer to the camera and grinned. "I've got an exciting surprise for you! Today, I'm whipping up the first batch of a new candle. It's a family recipe that's been passed down for generations. I won't reveal everything. Just know this candle has many uses—from seeing a person for who they truly are, to becoming the person you've always wanted to be." She clapped her hands together. "Tune back in later for the final reveal!"

"Wonder what kind of candle that is," Zoie said, sliding the phone in her pocket, "and did she steal it from Rosemary?"

"Sounds like it," Needles said. *"Could be Pyra was done playing second fiddle to Rosemary, and so she got rid of her once and for all, then stole her recipes for herself."*

I nodded. "I agree. I remember on Thursday, Rosemary was telling Pyra to just wait. Her time would come, but she still needed to learn more about the craft."

I'd just pulled up to Pyra's house when my phone rang.

Turning off the engine, I grabbed my phone and put it on speaker. "This is Agent Loci-Stone."

"Agent Loci-Stone," a female voice said, anger biting out her words. "This is Amber Redman."

I sighed. "I'm sorry for not calling you earlier. I assume you heard about the candle shop? I understand you're the new owner now. Listen, I'll tell you everything when I can, but right now, I need to take care of something important. It's about your sister's murder."

There was a moment of silence before Amber spoke up. "I actually have no idea what you're talking about when you say something happened to the shop. I've spoken to a lawyer and your husband, so I understand the shop is mine, but that's not why I'm calling. I'm calling to let you know someone has stolen pages out of our family grimoire." Once again, her tone was bitter and angry. "I *knew* this would happen if I didn't get to it sooner. Many of the recipes were created by my great-grandmother for specific circumstances. That's how I knew Rosemary had the grimoire. When one of her candle designs went viral, it was a specific design and result that *only* my family knew about. It's the same for the recipe that's missing. It blends and reveals auras."

Zoie inhaled sharply, and I could tell by her wide eyes she was thinking about the same thing I was—the video we'd just watched where Pyra had hinted about that very candle!

"Okay," I said, opening the door and motioning for Zoie to do the same. "Again, I'll figure this out the minute I take care of what I'm about to do. In fact, if I'm correct, you'll probably get the pages back shortly." I jogged to Pyra's front door. "But I really need to go now, Amber." I didn't wait for her to respond, disconnecting instead, and sliding the phone in my pocket. "Just follow my lead. Both of you. It could be Pyra admits everything without a fight."

Needles snorted, his wings glowing red and gold. *"Wishful thinking, Princess."*

But he settled on my shoulder without further argument.

I knocked on the door and waited...but when Pyra didn't answer, I knocked again and rang the doorbell.

"Want me to take a look?" Needles asked as he leaped from my shoulder.

"Yes. Zoie, go around and see if you can't detect anything. Watch your back."

They both took off in separate directions—Zoie around the side of the house, and Needles to the chimney. Incredibly, they both returned about the same time.

"Kick in the door, Shayla!" Zoie said as she sprinted around the corner. "Something's wrong."

On impulse, I reached out and opened the door. I'm not sure who was more surprised, Zoie or me, when the door pushed open.

"Ready your magic," I said. "We sweep first."

Nodding, Zoie stepped inside behind me, Needles hovering near my shoulder. Once we did a quick sweep, and I was sure no one was in the small cottage, Zoie led me to where she'd seen Pyra through the back window.

Two things assaulted me when I stepped inside the kitchen—the smell of sage and lavender, and the dead body of Pyra Thornby slumped over the kitchen table, a wick dipper protruding from her neck.

"Looks like we found the missing grimoire pages," Zoie said as we stared down at the table.

"Do you think Amber Redman is behind this?" Needles asked.

Zoie nodded. "I have to wonder if she hasn't been playing us this entire time as well."

"Then why not take the pages?" I mused. "Why leave them here and call us?"

"To throw us off?" Zoie said. "She waits until we are here to call and tell us. Could be she was watching for us. Plus, she had access to the shop these last few weeks. Maybe that's when she planted the candle."

I levitated the pages in the air and quickly scanned the sheets. The thing about a spell is that it's specific to the person casting it. He or she will add their own personal touch to enhance their creation. I winced when I saw Pyra had scratched out certain ingredients and added her own. While still able to read the original ingredients, I was sure Amber wouldn't be happy with the destruction of a family heirloom.

Of course, if she turned out to be the killer, then I guess it wouldn't matter.

"Come look at this, Shayla," Zoie said. "It's…odd. But kinda cool."

I lowered the papers and went to stand in front of the candle burning on the table. One side of the flame was bright red, while the other side was a vibrant emerald green. I'd never seen anything like it before. I put my hand over the flame and was shocked to discover it wasn't hot…but cold!

"Why does it smell like Alice's sage and lavender in here?" Zoie asked. "It's not coming from the candle. What did the killer do, light a candle while killing Pyra?"

I closed my eyes and thought about everything we knew so far about the suspects that were left. I thought about their motives, their opportunity…and then it clicked.

I opened my eyes. "Zoie, call your dad and let him know what's going on here with Pyra. I need him immediately. I'll call

Doc so he and Finn can get here as well. You and I have somewhere to be."

"Does this mean you know who the killer is, Princess?" Needles asked, his wings glowing purple and green.

I grinned. "I know who the killer is."

24

"You're sure you don't need backup?" Alex said through my speaker as I parked in the side alleyway.

"Zoie and I have this," I said. "Needles begged me to bring you in, but I vetoed him."

Alex chuckled as Needles vehemently denied my allegations from the backseat.

"We're here," I said. "I'll call you shortly when we have her apprehended."

"Be safe." Alex cleared his throat. "Zoie, watch your back."

"Will do, Daddy." Zoie disconnected and set down my phone.

"Let's go." I opened the driver's side door and waited until Needles flew out. "As we drove by just now, I noticed the CLOSED sign on her door. Let's go around back and see if she's in her apartment."

As we ascended the stairs, I motioned for Zoie to be on guard. The apartment door was open. It wasn't until I was a few feet from the door that my heart dropped. There were two sets of voices coming from inside—one belonging to our killer, the other to an elderly witch.

"I don't understand, Dana," the woman said. "Where are you going on such short notice?"

"I don't have time to explain right now, Miss Lotus," Dana said. "I just need to get away for a few days. I'll let you know when I'm back. Until then, if anyone comes around asking for me, tell them you don't know where I am."

"That's the truth. Because I *don't* know where you are going. And you're scaring me."

"Sorry, Miss Lotus. But you gotta go now."

I turned to Zoie. "I want you to fly to the other side of the building. Just listen in through the open window. You'll know when to strike. The perfect scenario would be for you to break the window or something to draw a distraction, but we'll play it by ear."

"You know I'll draw attention to myself, right? It's one thing for a gargoyle to fly around in the sky, it's another thing when I'm just hovering outside a window two stories up, peeking inside."

I let out a small laugh. "Yeah. Just do your best."

Zoie shifted and flew over the roof as Needles settled between my hair and neck.

I stepped inside the apartment. "You're not going anywhere, Dana."

"Damnit!" Dana snarled as she reached out and yanked the elderly witch to her chest...a wick dipper pressed against Miss Lotus' neck. "No closer, or I'll stick her. I've done it twice already."

"What's going on, Dana. I don't understand." Tears formed in the older witch's eyes. "This isn't like you."

"Shut up, Miss Lotus, and everything will be okay," Dana

hissed. "I just need you to get me out of here, and then I'll let you go when I'm off the island."

"It's ridiculous how many bad guys think they can actually leave the island," Needles murmured in my ear.

"It's Pyra's fault she's dead," Dana said. "She made that stupid video this morning, bragging and showing off!"

"Who killed Rosemary?" I said. "Was it you or Pyra?"

"Does it matter?"

"It matters to me."

Dana snorted. "I did. And the best part was, Pyra had no idea! She wasn't faking her surprise when she learned of the murder."

"Oh, Dana," Miss Lotus whimpered. "I can't believe you had anything to do with this."

"Why kill Rosemary?" I asked, wanting to keep Dana talking until Zoie could find her time to strike. "Was it because of the candles you and she were supposed to make?"

Rage flashed in Dana's eyes. "She *stole* that idea from me! During one of our sessions, she told me she had access to an aura candle in her family grimoire. I suggested we combine it with therapeutic healing powers. It would take a powerful spell, but I was sure we could do it."

"How exactly would the candle work?" I asked, though I was pretty sure I knew since I'd seen it in action twice already today—once on her desk and the other at Pyra's house.

"You light the candle, and the flame takes on the color of your aura. The candle will then read that aura and decide what it is you need to balance out. It would then emit that smell."

"That's actually quite clever," Needles said.

Dana's nostrils flared. "But then Rosemary dropped the aura idea and just made therapeutic candles! Cutting me out!"

I nodded and tried to sound sympathetic. "And so when

Rosemary recanted her offer to partner with you, you decided to kill her?"

"Yes!" Dana shouted. "I convinced Pyra to go into partnership with me. She wasn't near as powerful a witch as Rosemary, but it wouldn't matter as long as we had the aura spell from Rosemary's grimoire. I convinced Pyra to steal the pages."

"Then why go to Rosemary's store and make that scene on Thursday morning?" I asked, honestly confused.

"Because Pyra called me Wednesday night to say she was having second thoughts. I admit, I was angry. I was *sure* Rosemary had convinced Pyra to stay on, and so I went to the store and made a little scene. Not my finest move. But Pyra had already given me a prototype of a candle she'd been working on earlier in the week, so I knew it worked! What Pyra didn't give me was a copy of the grimoire pages!" She took a step backward, dragging Miss Lotus closer to the open window. "So I went back into Wicked Wicks Thursday afternoon right before the store was due to close and left that note for Rosemary, asking her to meet me there at 7:30 so we could talk. She was with a customer, so she just acknowledged me from afar…she didn't see I had on gloves. Otherwise, she might have been suspicious." She let out a small laugh. "I was a little surprised when she let me in that night, to be honest. But I was smart. I brought greasy takeout along so she'd have to take it out to the trash bin outside. I knew she wouldn't want the smell to linger all night around her candles. When she went outside, I followed her out, and then killed her with one of my wick dippers. My plan was to drag her back inside the shop and leave her, but the ice cream truck was just sitting right there."

"And the lavender and sage?" I mused.

"I bought a couple candles and essential oil from Alice's store a while back. I knew it was a scent only they carried and sold. So I came to Rosemary's store Thursday night prepared. I was going to stash the body in the store to frame Pyra, but also rub beeswax and essential oil on Rosemary's clothes to point to Alice."

Miss Lotus whimpered. "So when you came by Thursday to bring me dinner, that wasn't you being nice. It was to give you an alibi?"

"Sure was," Dana said. "Sorry about that."

Only, she didn't sound sorry.

Dana shook her head and scraped the wick dipper along Miss Lotus' neck. "It wasn't until I spoke to Pyra on Friday afternoon that I got the feeling she was trying to do the same thing Rosemary had done. Use me and then toss me aside! My plan was to burn the place enough it would leave her without a job. Then she'd have to bring me in." She stopped moving the wick dipper, her hand tightening on the weapon. "Pyra called me Friday and asked if I killed Rosemary." She let out a bark of laughter. "Yeah, like I'm just going to come out and admit it. I said no, and she said she didn't kill her, either. And she started whining about how she was scared. So maybe I should just stay away for a while until everything gets settled. Maybe we'd talk about the aura candle in a couple weeks." She gripped the handle of the wick dipper so tightly now, her knuckles were white and Miss Lotus let out a cry of pain as the sharp hook of the wick dipper scratched her thin skin, causing blood to trickle. "So I try to play it calm. I tell Pyra that's fine. I understand. But I'd like to talk to her about Rosemary's death because I was feeling conflicted as well. After all, the last thing I said to Rosemary on Thursday was awful. I asked if we could maybe meet at the candle store later that night because I'd like to buy a candle to ease my guilt." She let out a maniacal laugh. "She said I could come by around 7:15, and she'd let me in."

That all was true. We'd witnessed it during our stakeout.

She took another step back toward the window, dragging a pale, bleeding Miss Lotus with her. "What Pyra didn't realize was that I had embedded a firestarter spell inside a candle I'd made, set to go off hours later when the shop was closed. I hid it in my purse, and she never had a clue."

"Oh, Dana," Miss Lotus said. "I'm disappointed in you."

"Boo-hoo," Dana sneered. "So, anyway, while I was inside the store browsing and buying last night, I left the spelled candle behind. Leaving me totally in the clear." She shrugged, her hand slipping and once again drawing blood from Miss Lotus. "Unfortunately, something went wrong and the candle didn't go off a few hours later, but like sixteen hours later."

"Let me gut her right here, Princess! She could have harmed the twins!"

Just the thought of that had me seeing red. "You're damn lucky the twins are advanced witches and put that fire out!"

"Like I said, it wasn't meant to burn the place down...just damage it enough to close down for a while." She narrowed her eyes. "Besides, Pyra shouldn't have tried to double-cross me. It was her fault!" She took another step backward. "But then that stupid witch went and posted a bragging video of the new candle she was making." She let out a shaky breath. "I knew what that meant. She had to go. I didn't need the physical grimoire pages. I just needed a photo. So I went to her place over lunch, armed with a wick dipper and some of Alice's candles and essential oil and let myself in. Pyra didn't even know I was there. Never saw it coming." She took one last step backward and hit the windowsill. "And now, Miss Lotus and I are going to levitate ourselves down and take a ride. I promise to let her go when I feel it's safe."

"Where are you going to go?" I asked. "This is an island. It's not like you can just get in a car and drive away."

"It's a large island when you need to hide out," Dana argued. "I'll wait until the time is right, steal a boat, and you'll never hear from me again."

I glanced outside and saw Zoie hovering near the window. "Or maybe we just end this right here and now."

With a small nod of my head, Zoie kicked in the window, causing the glass to shatter. Miss Lotus let out a startled cry, and Dana turned on instinct.

It was all the distraction I needed.

When Dana had turned, the wick dipper moved a few inches away from Miss Lotus' neck.

Needles shot out from under my hair, a quill in each front paw and wings glowing purple and green. *"I'll grab the weapon, Princess!"*

Dana turned back around just in time to see Needles heading straight for her, his quills whipping through the air. They made contact with her wrist and hands, opening her skin and making her bleed. With a cry of surprise and pain, Dana let go of the wick dipper.

"Miss Lotus, move!" I shouted, as I raised my hands and dropped to my knees.

While Dana batted her hands at Needles, magic sparking and dying at her fingertips, Zoie ran up behind Dana, grabbed her hands, and wrestled them behind her back. I sent a jolt of magic to Dana's knees, causing her to cry out, buckle, and drop to the floor.

I scrambled to my feet. "Stand back, Zoie!"

The minute she jumped up, I reached for the Binder around my waist and threw it at Dana, immediately encircling her in a magic bubble that stripped her of her magical abilities.

"You okay, Miss Lotus?" I asked, hurrying to kneel in front of her on the floor.

"Yes," she said, struggling to her feet as Zoie and I helped her up. "Just sad, dear."

"Well, I'm as happy as a porcupine in a barrel of pretzels!" He whipped his quills through the air in front of the bubble Dana was captured in. *"This moment would only be better if I could carve the twins' names on her."*

25

"*The twins are already here!*"
"*So are the others.*"
"*The cake is so beautiful.*"
"*I bet it'll taste like cotton candy!*"
"*Black Forest King is excited too!*"

The fireflies were eagerly circling my head as Mr. Pine lifted his heavy branches for Alex and me to enter Black Forest. Needles zipped ahead, the fireflies chasing after him.

"*There are many already here, Princess,*" Mr. Pine said. "*Enjoy your night.*"

Alex and I ducked and entered the forest. And like always, the magic of the forest rushed through my body. Alex grabbed my hand, and we hurried toward the party.

I laughed as a rabbit dashed across our path. "I think all the forest animals are out tonight."

Before long, Alex and I reached the clearing where Dad stood…tall and proud. Usually he was enough to capture my attention, but tonight, I had a sudden flashback to the last big party we'd had here.

The night Alex and I had gotten married.

"Brings back the best night of my life," Alex murmured, drawing me close for a quick kiss. "The night you said yes to being my wife."

Dominic had outdone himself as the party planner. Enchanted strings of fairy lights were draped artfully through the lower branches of Black Forest, creating a canopy of soft, warm light. He'd used moss, mushrooms, and wildflowers to create natural centerpieces on the tables scattered around the clearing.

"Look, Shayla!" Zoie called when she spotted us. "Dominic made wearable wreaths!" She laughed as she slammed a circle of daisies and baby's breath down on her head before trying to do the same to Harlow—who was having none of it.

I waved at Mom, who was leaning against Dad's trunk, one of his massive branches stroking her back. Serena, Tamara, and Pepper were setting out the cake and refreshments, while Aunt Starla and Walt helped arrange presents.

Grant and Tommy were entertaining the kids by blowing enchanted bubbles that popped in the air and rained down confetti on everyone. A huge hit if the peals of laughter were any indication.

"I hear you got your killer," GiGi said, wrapping an arm around me and pulling me in for a hug. "I knew you would."

I breathed her in, then turned to Byron. "Sorry Alex and I had to bail on you guys for dinner the other night."

"Perfectly understandable," Byron said.

"I'd have thought for sure it was Alice Ashton," GiGi said. "She's always been a little unstable."

"This is stellar," Finn said as she and Jordan sidled up next to Alex and me. "Best one-year-old party I've ever been to."

Jordan laughed. "Me too."

I nodded and looked around at all our family and friends. "I'd have to say, it's probably the best I've been to as well."

The fireflies chattered excitedly as they buzzed between clusters of sugary cotton candy and honey-coated berries.

"Don't eat so much you all get sick!" Needles bellowed.

The lightning bugs just giggled and scattered, thin threads of pink swirling around them as they quickly shared and gobbled down the cotton candy.

"I also think it's cool Tommy is here," Finn said. "I'm glad to see him so happy with Pepper and her kids."

"He's a natural," I agreed.

The bubbles were over, and now Tommy was putting his massive troll-like body to use by letting the kids climb all over him like he was a tree.

I excused myself from the group, hurrying over to greet Mom and Dad. Levitating myself up onto Dad's huge tree roots, I greeted them both.

"Everything looks amazing," I said, wrapping Mom in a hug.

"It does, doesn't it?" Mom gushed. "This is the first birthday party Black Forest has seen in…"

"In too many years," Dad finished. *"Hello, Daughter of my Heart. I have missed you."*

I wrapped my arms around Dad's trunk and brushed my cheek against his rough bark. "Hey, Dad. Thanks for letting us do this here."

"I have enjoyed watching all the kids chase the bubbles and confetti." He chuckled. *"Being surrounded by so many family and friends has made my heart full tonight."*

"I should probably go see if anyone needs help," I said.

"Everyone gather round!" Dominic called. "It's time to get the party started!"

"Guess that's my cue," I said, lowering myself back to the forest floor.

Dominic clapped his hands together, and all the kids stopped what they were doing and ran to him as I grabbed Alex's hand and dragged him behind me.

"Ic! Ic!" the twins chanted.

"Wait for me!" Needles said, his wings glowing purple and green.

Gifts were unwrapped, goodie bags were handed out, and soon it was time for cake and ice cream. Tamara had designed the two-tier cake to mimic the forest—in honor of the twins. The bottom tier was decorated to look like a mossy forest floor, with tiny, edible mushrooms and flowers glowing faintly along the edges. Delicate fondant trees, ferns, and vines wrapped around the base of the cake. The top tier featured myriad woodland animals, each one crafted with exquisite detail. A fox curled around a rabbit, while a squirrel held an acorn close to its chest. Tamara had added extra enchantments to the animals as well—the rabbit's nose would twitch, or the squirrel would shift its tiny paws.

There was even a flying porcupine.

"That's the most gorgeous cake I've ever seen," Pepper whispered. "I'm going to have to hire you ladies to make my kids' cakes from here on out."

Serena and Tamara both laughed.

Grant and Serena set the twins in highchairs, then presented them with their own individual baby cakes designed to look like the big cake Tamara had made. Serena had worked her own magic into the design, just like Tamara.

"Don't forget the candle!" Dominic exclaimed, running to get the special candle Rosemary Redman had made for the twins' main cake.

Once lit, everyone oohed and aahed at the magic and music the candle emitted.

"Surely they won't light the little cakes," Needles said, seconds before Grant stuck a skinny candle into each of the twins' cakes. *"This is it. The night Black Forest burns."*

Alex chuckled as he slipped his hand into mine. A couple times already, Serena's dragon side had manifested out of the twins. Like Serena, they couldn't shift, but they could manipulate and breathe fire. Once the twins' candles were lit, we all sang happy birthday. And when Serena and Grant told the twins to blow out their candles…

Instead of a puff of air shooting out of their mouths… smoke billowed and rolled, causing the twins to squeal in laughter.

Dad's chuckle reverberated in my head. *"Clever and powerful."*

"Those are *my* great-grandkids!" GiGi called out proudly.

* * *

"This has been a great night," Mom said a little while later as the party wound down.

The kids had all crashed and were now being carried out of Black Forest by their parents. Dominic, Harlow, Zoie, Alex, and I had volunteered to clean up. With our combined magic, it wouldn't take long.

"It *has* been a great night," I agreed, using my magic to clear a table.

"You gonna stay a little later and talk with your dad?" Alex asked once we finished cleaning.

"Do you mind?" I asked, leaning into his chest.

"Not at all." He wrapped his arms around me and kissed my

temple. "Needles will keep you company on your journey back to the castle."

I glanced over at the sleeping porcupine. Like the fireflies, he'd had a little too much sugar and was now crashing atop one of dad's branches.

"We're finished as well," Zoie called out.

I kissed Alex goodnight and smiled as he slung an arm around his daughter and led her, Harlow, and Dominic out of Black Forest.

"I should go as well," Mom said. "It's been a long day for me. I'm glad you solved your case." She kissed me, said goodnight to Dad, and made her way to the entrance of Black Forest.

"It is now just us, Daughter of my Heart," Dad said. *"Even Needles has drifted off."*

I chuckled and sat down at the base of his trunk, pressing my back against him. "I can't stay long. I'm exhausted too."

"Harlow's friend, Dominic, did an amazing job tonight."

I grinned. "He did. The twins absolutely love him. Harlow is going to have to keep him around no matter what now."

Dad chuckled. *"I saw the way they interacted. I have a feeling he is not going anywhere."*

"At least not until GiGi finishes with his ice cream truck."

"What is this?" Dad asked.

"So with the dead body being discovered in *Frozen Dreams*, Harlow was sure no one would want their kid getting ice cream from Dominic anymore. At least, not from that truck. So GiGi said she'd take it and make it so it never happened."

"And just how is your grandmother going to do that?"

I grinned. "I have no idea, but I'm sure it will be spectacular."

"And the sister of the young woman who was murdered," Dad mused. *"What will she do?"*

"I spoke to Amber earlier, and she has decided to stay on Enchanted Island and run the candle shop. Her sister left her everything—the house, store, all of it."

"I suppose that is good, then."

We were quiet for a while, and I was about to wish him goodnight...when Needles came zipping toward us, his wings glowing purple and green.

"Well?" Needles demanded. *"Did you ask her? Is she or isn't she?"*

"Who are you speaking of, old friend?" Dad asked.

I shook my head and laughed. "Needles wanted me to ask Serena if she was pregnant or not."

"Don't even say it aloud, Princess! We don't want that whispered into the universe!"

"Well, I didn't ask, so you'll just have to wait and see."

"Do you have a guess?" Dad mused.

I shrugged. "I honestly don't know. She didn't say anything, but I watched her tonight, and I have my suspicions."

Needles clutched his chest and gasped...then slowly drifted down to the forest floor like he was dead. *"I cannot take it, Black Forest King."*

Dad and I both laughed.

"No matter the outcome, Needles," I said, "you will be happy for her."

"Perhaps we should speak of something else before my quills all fall out," Needles suggested as he zipped to my shoulder.

"Okay," I said. "How about GiGi's upcoming wedding? It's just two months away. She's planning a bachelorette party a week after Alex and I celebrate our one-year anniversary next month."

"Where are we going?" Needles asked, his wings glowing purple and green. *"I'm ready for anything!"*

DEADLY FLAME

Dad chuckled. *"I am sure it is like Alex and Shayla's honeymoon, old friend. You will probably not be invited to a girls' party."*

I narrowed my eyes at Needles. "Dad's right. You're not invited."

Needles made a weird sound with his mouth and waved a paw in the air. *"Nonsense. I was told I couldn't go on your honeymoon…and I did!"*

"As a stowaway!" I exclaimed.

"So?" Needles pressed. *"Where are we going?"*

* * *

Are you ready for the next book in the series? Then click here and get *Deadly Mansion* and find out what secrets await Shayla, GiGi, and the rest of the gang at GiGi's bachelorette party. Deadly Mansion

* * *

Do you love the PADA world as much as I do? The PADA world encompasses many series. Here is the order in which you CAN read them. You don't have to read in this order, it's simply a guide to give you an idea on where to start! Did you know the A Witch in the Woods series is what started it all?

The Paranormal Apprehension and Detention Agency World:

1. A Witch in the Woods: *Deadly Claws* Deadly Claws

2. Kara Hilder Mystery: *Sounds of Murder Sounds of Murder*
3. Enchanted Waters: *Tangled Waters Tangled Waters*
4. Isle of Enchantment: *Mystic Lies Mystic Lies*

Thank you for spending time in this magical world!

Also, if you want to keep in touch with what's releasing AND find out more about me and my real-family and our crazy antics, sign up for my newsletter and get a FREE boxset of The Enchanted Island Mysteries: Serena & Grant! This is a prequel to it all! Just click here: http://jennastjames.com/.

Are you on Facebook? So am I! You can find me two places:
Jenna's Reading Crew: https://www.facebook.com/groups/2787636591248452

Paranormal Cozy Mystery Coven: https://www.facebook.com/groups/paranormalcozymystery

Bookbub: https://www.bookbub.com/profile/jenna-st-james

. . .

Blessings, my dear readers!!

Made in United States
Cleveland, OH
02 May 2025